How the Scot Stole the Bride

D1563875

How the Scot Stole the Bride

Laura A. Barnes

Laura A. Barnes

2021

Copyright © 2021 by Laura A. Barnes

All rights reserved. This book or any portion thereof may not be reproduced or used in any manner whatsoever without the express written permission of the publisher except for the use of brief quotations in a book review or scholarly journal.

First Printing: 2021

ISBN: 9798535015262

Laura A. Barnes

Website: www.lauraabarnes.com

Cover Art by Cheeky Covers

Editor: Telltail Editing

To: My lovely reviewers

I place my heart and soul into your hands and hope you love the stories as much as I loved writing them. And you always offer me the kindest words of support with your wonderful reviews. I thank each and every one of you for taking this journey with me. I hope to share many more stories with you.

Cast of Characters

Hero ~ Duncan Forrester

Heroine ~ Selina Pemberton

Uncle Theo ~ Duke of Colebourne

Lucas Gray ~ Colebourne's son

Susanna Forrester ~ Colebourne's sister-in-law/Duncan's mother

Ramsay Forrester ~ Lady Forrester's husband/Duncan's father

Jacqueline Holbrooke ~ Colebourne's niece

Charlotte Holbrooke ~ Colebourne's niece

Jasper Sinclair ~ Charlotte's husband

Evelyn Holbrooke ~ Colebourne's niece

Reese Worthington ~ Evelyn's husband

Gemma Holbrooke ~ Colebourne's niece

Abigail Cason ~ Colebourne's ward

Duke of Norbury ~ Selina Pemberton's father

Chapter One

Selina Pemberton stared at the altar with a wistful expression. If one felt a variety of emotions simultaneously, then she experienced them in full today. While she watched her new friend Gemma Holbrooke marry Lord Ralston this morning, Selina felt such joy for them. However, she also watched the ceremony with bittersweet irony.

She sat in between her fiancé, Lord Gray, and her future father-in-law, the Duke of Colebourne, during the ceremony. The former was the bride's cousin and the latter her uncle. Since they were set to wed within a month's time, it only seemed fitting for Selina to sit with the bride's family. Her father sat on the other side of Lord Gray.

A smile tugged at Selina's lips, remembering Gemma's enthusiasm when she spoke her vows. The bride hadn't been able to contain her excitement at becoming Lady Ralston. The groom had chuckled his amusement and gazed at his bride with adoration. When they spoke their wedding vows, love shined from their gazes, and every single lady sighed, wishing for the same. When the couple shared a kiss, groans from the gentleman soon joined the sighs in the chapel.

One would think Selina, who was about to become a bride herself, barely contained her own excitement for her impending marriage. Well, that was where the bittersweetness came into play with her strung-out emotions. And let's not forget the irony of the event. No, it was the major feature of the dilemma she had found herself in, one she held no clue how to remove herself from. Her time to call off the betrothal her father committed her to when she was but a babe still in the nursery ticked away.

A commitment her father reminded her of constantly. A commitment Selina had never wanted and dreaded with each day drawing nearer. A commitment making all parties involved miserable. A commitment uniting two powerful dukedoms into one.

Selina and Lucas Gray were the only children born into a ducal family. Their marriage would make their family the most powerful and richest in England once they spoke their vows. Any offspring would only build upon their dynasty.

A chill shivered along Selina's spine at the thought of Lucas Gray bedding her. She held no attraction toward the marquess. Their relationship wasn't even on friendly terms. Gray tolerated her at best, and only when his father encouraged him to. In truth, the fault didn't lie with Gray, but with her. Selina had made it complicated for Gray or any member of his family to find anything likable about her. No, she had tormented his cousins over the years with her shrewish behavior and acted the pampered princess while in his presence. Her behavior of late had only been more vindictive once her father started pressuring Colebourne to set a wedding date.

Selina had hoped the more obnoxious she acted, the more it would force Gray to break the betrothal. However, he wouldn't budge in his duty to fulfill his father's word. No matter how much he wished the same as Selina. He held no love for her. And there was where the rest of the irony came into play. Lucas Gray had already lost his heart to another, the very same lady who stood next to Gemma throughout the wedding ceremony. Abigail Cason.

While their own wedding drew nearer, one would think Gray and Selina would have watched the ceremony holding hands, anxiously waiting for their own special day. No. Gray kept a distance from Selina and never once glanced her way. His stare had remained focused on Abigail since the ceremony began. And once the ceremony ended, he remained at the young miss's side during the celebration, abandoning Selina once again. Colebourne tried to mask his son's boorish behavior with his own courteous attention, but it didn't help to soothe Selina's temperament. She was on the verge of acting vindictively and needed to remove herself before she acted on her emotions like she had with her previous behavior.

At one time, she would have made a catty remark about Abigail's standing in society to seek her revenge. However, Selina was attempting to right the wrongs of her past. But standing by with a smile pasted on her face while her fiancé devoted his attention to another lady was more than Selina wished to endure. The stares filled with pity she received from the members of Gray's family and other wedding guests ignited the fuel for revenge. Instead of striking out, Selina bit her tongue and removed herself from the situation, a tactic she learned to save herself from Lucas's wrath and the coldness of his family.

So instead of enjoying the wedding brunch, she found herself back in the chapel, contemplating how to find the courage to continue with the journey her father demanded of her. What her true heart desired didn't matter. Her desires, wants, needs would never find fulfillment. Her dreams must remain fantasies to indulge in whenever life became unbearably lonely. It was a state she'd spent her entire life in and would continue to endure if she married Gray.

A single tear leaked from her eye, trailing down her cheek to land on her clasped hands. It landed on the finger that soon would hold a wedding ring. Selina choked back a sob at the symbolism.

"Tears, lass? Picturing your own wedding, are ye?"

Selina stiffened at the Scottish brogue. There was only one Scot who taunted her with his slanderous tongue. At every opportunity, the heathen would seek her out to aggravate. She fooled herself into believing today would be any different. Just because she had formed a friendship with Gemma didn't mean the rest of Gray's family felt any differently toward her. Duncan Forrester included.

She drew a deep breath to slow her pounding heart and lifted her hand to swipe at her damp cheek. Selina wished to avoid him today, but it would appear the universe would once again deny her a favor. She had managed to stay out of his reach since their horrible encounter a few weeks before. The only highlight she gained was Colebourne's guidance and Lady Forrester's kindness. Lady Forrester paid her more friendly affections than her own son.

No. Lady Forrester's son turned Selina into a frenzied shrew whenever he cornered her. If he wasn't turning her into a shrew, then he turned her emotions into a quivering mess of unrequited lust. He left her aching to explore the possibilities of where their passion could lead. Not only were they foolish, but her wanton thoughts would only lead Selina toward a scandal, one she could never recover from.

She supposed, in time, if she acted on her impulses and engaged with Forrester on the passions he tempted her with, they could weather the storm their union would create. The temptation to indulge in the sin beckoned her. However, Forrester was Gray's cousin. That fact alone made

Selina push her urges as deeply as she could into the unknown. She must never act upon them, no matter how much his kisses set her soul on fire.

She rolled her shoulders back before lifting her gaze. "As a matter of fact, I am. I was picturing Lucas speaking his vows while clutching my hand. I am looking forward to the day, and the emotion overwhelmed me."

"Do you still believe the wedding will actually occur?" Forrester arched a brow.

Selina smiled with confidence. "Colebourne has set a date, and the invitations were delivered this week. What more proof will it take for you to believe it will happen?"

Duncan snorted. "Do you hold the belief Gray will make you his bride because Colebourne has given his authorization and a few measly invites were delivered? You, my dear, are so gullible."

Selina bit the inside of her cheek to keep her temper in check. She refused to rise to his bait. Every time she had in the past, she'd ended up in his arms, and he'd kissed her so thoroughly she walked away dreaming of a different outcome for her life.

She must resist the temptation, even when her body begged otherwise.

Selina slipped her gloves back on and rose from the bench, walking toward Forrester. She pretended to brush off a speck of lint from his suit, her hand curving across his shoulder and sliding along his arm. Her hand brushed lightly across his when she leaned in toward him. She inhaled his woodsy scent, her insides sparking to life.

She stood on her tiptoes and whispered in his ear, "No, you barbaric Scot, you are the gullible one. I will not only wed Lucas Gray in a few weeks, but I also will become his bride in every way it matters too."

"Like hell," he gritted between his teeth.

Selina chuckled, pushing Forrester out of her way. "Tsk, tsk. Such language in the lord's house. But then I should expect this behavior from the likes of you."

Selina walked away before he responded. Only she never made it out of the chapel before Forrester came upon her. He turned her around and backed Selina against the door. An unnamed emotion singed her soul from the intensity in his stare. Her confidence in walking away from him dissolved into a quivering mess of desire. Her soul knew he meant to devour her lips before her mind comprehended his intentions. Selina's body betrayed her with their actions.

Her arms wrapped around his neck, urging his lips to hers, while her tongue licked her lips in anticipation. She pressed herself closer to him, needing his heat to consume her. Forrester needed no encouragement. He stole the very breath from her soul when his mouth descended onto hers.

The fiery licks of the forbidden teased her lips apart to invade her mouth with each enflamed stroke of his tongue against hers. Duncan's kiss was relentless in its quest to brand her as his. He showed Selina no mercy with his onslaught of passionate need. His embrace tightened, pulling Selina closer when she melted against him. At her every moan, he captured the vibration and drew forth her surrender. She hung on the brink of capitulating herself to the pleasure of his kisses when he abruptly pulled away.

Forrester dropped his arms and stepped back, leaving Selina grasping for something to cling to. Her trembling hand clasped onto the door handle while she fought with her legs not to give out. Their gazes clashed, and she sucked in a gasp. If she thought his gaze was intense before their kiss, it held nothing to the possessive stare gliding over her body.

His lips snarled into a determined smile, leaving Selina no doubt of his intentions. "As I said before, like hell, *Duchess*."

Chapter Two

Duncan stalked into his bedroom with the same fury consuming him since he left Selina. Selina with her eyes wide, in shock at him acting like a barbarian at his finest. However, it wasn't only shock gleaming from her eyes, but the same state of need coursing through his veins.

As much as she continued to deny their attraction, Selina Pemberton wanted him.

The pull of her fingers in his hair when he devoured her lips. The pull of her lips when she matched him stroke for stroke. The pull of her moans into his soul. All those signs spoke otherwise. And like always, he'd tried to force her to admit her feelings.

When would he ever learn to approach her differently? Every time he witnessed her fragile struggle to hold herself together and please everyone around her, he only wanted to strip her bare. He wanted her to acknowledge the mad attraction surrounding them. But most of all, he wanted Selina to make a choice: his cousin Lucas or him.

Duncan slumped into a chair, bringing the bottle of whiskey to his lips. He drank a long swallow followed by another before lowering the bottle. The dark liquid stained the light fabric of his suit coat when he swiped his lips with his arm. A bitter laugh escaped his lips when he noticed not only the whiskey but the shade of Selina's lip color. He closed his eyes and slumped his head back against the chair.

The kiss they'd shared today played out before him. Every kiss they'd shared before then had been a distraction to cover for his cousins' mischiefs. The kiss today had been for him alone. He couldn't resist wiping away her smug confidence at securing a wedding date. His kiss was a warning: He would show no mercy in claiming her heart for himself.

Duncan went to great lengths to leave Selina, and she still invaded his sanity without even trying to. He'd fled from the chapel as if the hounds of hell were nipping at his heels. If he stayed one moment longer with Selina, he couldn't be held responsible for the scandal that would have surely happened. He'd stormed past his mother and uncle to his cousin Gemma and her new husband, Ralston. He ignored Gemma, not even congratulating her, and demanded a horse to borrow from Ralston. They both looked at him with confusion, but Ralston agreed. He had ridden hard back to London, stormed inside his uncle's townhome, startling the butler, Goodwin, and made another demand. He wanted a bottle of his uncle's finest whiskey. Goodwin shook his head and muttered about rude guests, procuring Duncan a bottle before walking away in disgust.

Duncan rose and stripped off his coat. Instead of throwing it across the room, he laid it gently over the arm of the chair. He divested himself of his vest, cravat, and boots. After undoing a few buttons of his shirt, he sat back down and drew his suit coat over his lap. With every draw from the bottle, he rubbed his fingers across the stain. The more he drank, the darker his thoughts turned. Not only dark, but perhaps a bit mad, too. He swore he felt a sizzle at every stroke over the shade of pink.

Was he mad to indulge in his fantasies of stealing Selina away from Lucas? He must end this obsession he had for the blonde vixen. His pursuit would only bring scandal to his family, who walked the line of propriety as it was. If word leaked of his cousins' indiscretions before they married their husbands, rumors would spread, making it impossible for Jacqueline and Abigail to find grooms. Abigail struggled as it was, due to her standing in society. While his family considered Abigail one of theirs, the fact of the matter was, she was a daughter of an unwed servant. Uncle Theo might have raised her as his niece, but she wasn't.

No. Duncan couldn't risk their reputations for a simple infatuation. No matter how much he desired to make Selina his. He couldn't hurt his family with another one of his foolish antics. While his own father found humor in his prowess pursuits, his Uncle Theo didn't deserve to have his plans for his only offspring ruined because Duncan couldn't control an itch. An itch he had countless offers to scratch. Why he denied himself the pleasure of indulging in those offers was beyond him.

Duncan laughed again and took another drink. Who did he try to fool? He had always been a sucker for the weak and vulnerable. Many viewed Selina as who she portrayed herself to be. A shrew, dragon, troublemaker. She was anything but. No, she was lonely, desperate for attention, and vulnerable. It was her vulnerability that drew Duncan toward her, pulling him deeper under her spell. To show Selina she was loved was his only purpose.

She deserved love more than anyone he knew, Duncan included. A loving family surrounded him, he had more friends than he could count, and he shared more bedsheets with women he only wanted to forget. Yet Selina had no one. Even her own father regarded her as a prize for the highest bidder to win. It wasn't until the last few weeks that his cousin Gemma had befriended her, and his own mother had taken Selina under her wing. In fact, his mother carried on about how wonderful Lady Selina was. The rest of his family still refused to embrace her. They kept her at arm's length, waiting for her to strike. Yet she hadn't. She smiled with the grace of a true duchess, displaying her patience through every snide remark. Pride didn't even begin to describe what he held for her.

Duchess. He'd taken to calling her that lately to emphasize her status if she became Lucas's wife. Selina would become a duchess after Uncle Theo died if she married his cousin. If, the magic word. She would make an elegant duchess. It was a role she had prepared her entire life for. A role her father expected her to fulfill. A role most befitting for Selina. One she had been born into. But could he destroy the destiny that had been laid at her feet?

No.

With a deep sigh, he rose and set the bottle to the side. He pulled his valise out from underneath the bed and started to empty the contents of the dresser into it. In his current state, he wouldn't travel very far. He would leave at first light for home. He kept stumbling on the trek, back and forth across the room, gathering his belongings. Also, he couldn't leave without informing his mother of his plans.

A knock sounded at the door before it was flung open without permission to enter. He scowled at the intruder, his cousin Lucas.

"I wondered where you took off to. You left me to fend for myself at that fiasco. I had to dance with a bunch of old biddies, each of them demanding information of my own upcoming nuptials." Lucas spied the bottle of whiskey and took a drink before continuing. "Do you know how frustrating it is to keep up the pretense of liking my fiancée? Even after everything that has transpired, Father still insists on this union."

Duncan gritted his teeth, his hands curling into fists. While he usually had a carefree attitude, he now fought to rein in his temper. Lucas was more of a brother to him than a cousin, but even with their close ties, he fought to hold back from unleashing his fury. Lucas's pitiful display of wanting sympathy for his situation grated on Duncan's nerves. Lucas should feel nothing but gratitude for his father tethering him to Selina. The lucky bastard held a treasure within his grasp, but he couldn't see past his own misery to appreciate it.

Lucas narrowed his gaze. "Are you leaving?"

"Aye," Duncan grunted.

"Oh, no. You cannot."

Duncan shrugged his indifference and continued packing. He opened the wardrobe and, with one swipe, gathered his clothing. He kicked open his trunk, threw the clothes in the bottom, and turned to gather his footwear. When he turned back around, he smacked into Lucas, who held Duncan's clothes in his fold. Lucas marched past him and threw them back into the wardrobe. Duncan scowled, threw the footwear in the trunk, and went back for the clothes. Lucas stood in front of the wardrobe with his arms spread wide, a desperate, pleading look on his face.

"Move," Duncan snarled.

"No."

Duncan tried shoving Lucas, but Lucas stood firm. When he pushed Lucas in the shoulder, his hand landed in midair past Lucas, causing him to lose his balance. Perhaps he had drunk more than he thought. Lucas caught him and helped him back to the chair. Lucas acting in kindness only enflamed Duncan's rage. He glared at his cousin, his hands gripping the arms of the chair.

Lucas shook his head and settled into a chair with the whiskey in his clutch. It was a scene they had shared many times in the past, except this time it wasn't in a friendly manner on Duncan's part. However, his cousin was too selfish to see otherwise. Lucas kept to his ramblings over his impending marriage to Selina Pemberton and failed to notice how every derogatory comment only made Duncan angrier.

"Stop," Duncan demanded.

Lucas's mouth hung open, stopping his rant. It was then he noticed Duncan's agitated state. "What is the matter?"

Duncan arched a brow. "You are a fool."

"A fool?"

"Aye. A fool. You have a chance to marry a beauty. Once you say I do, you will have created a dynasty for your family to enjoy for centuries to come. Yet you sputter on about how unfair life is for you. A fool."

"If you believe I am so lucky, then you marry the shrew," Lucas scoffed.

Duncan flew out of his chair so fast, Lucas was unprepared for his attack. He landed on Lucas, toppling the chair over backward. When he swung out to clip Lucas on the chin, his cousin twisted his face away. Duncan's fist connected with the floor instead. His drunken state made him impaired with clumsy movements. Lucas shoved Duncan off him and straightened his clothing. He stared down at Duncan with a scowl, then relented, holding a hand down. He helped Duncan settle back into the chair.

"Not a shrew. She does not deserve the injustice your family treats her with," Duncan mumbled.

Lucas stared at Duncan in confusion. His gaze narrowed, then he nodded. His nod was his agreement with Duncan's demand. "Why are you leaving?"

"A lass I desire is set to marry another."

Lucas's gaze drilled into Duncan's. "Then fight for her."

"Cannot."

"Pshh. You, my friend, are Duncan Forrester. You can charm any lass away from any bloke within your reach."

Duncan blew out a sigh. "Not this lass or her bloke."

"Why not?"

"'Tis not possible without causing a scandal."

Lucas laughed. "As if causing a scandal ever stopped you before. Why let it stop you now?"

"I cannot explain. 'Tis best if I left."

"Can you at least wait until after my wedding? I need all the support I can get to carry through with my commitment," Lucas pleaded.

Duncan's fury disappeared at his cousin's heartfelt plea. While he planned to leave for selfish reasons, he couldn't abandon Lucas in his hour of need. Also, it would allow him to purge Selina Pemberton from his soul. After he watched her speak her vows, it would destroy anything he felt for her. The next few weeks would be a tortuous hell to endure, but one he must suffer from to move forward.

He nodded his acceptance.

"Thank you, cousin." Lucas gripped his shoulder.

Lucas headed out of the bedroom. Duncan thought he had left until Lucas's question caused Duncan to stiffen. "Is love what you feel for your lass?"

"Aye."

"Then do you not owe it to yourself and her to discover if it is worth enough to risk scandal for?"

Duncan turned in his seat to answer Lucas, but his cousin had disappeared. Were the feelings he held for the lass worth risking everything for a lifetime of everlasting love?

Chapter Three

Duncan strode into the breakfast room, not glancing at who sat around the table. As always, multiple conversations filled the room. He wasn't in the mood for his boisterous family. On a morning like today, he would have preferred the quietness of his own family's townhome. But his Uncle Theo, the Duke of Colebourne, insisted for him to stay with them during his time in London. Lucas's questions from the evening before left him much to contemplate.

He loaded his plate full of the scrumptious fare laid before him. With the food and the coffee he requested from the footman, his stomach would soon settle from his overindulgence. When he turned around to sit, Duncan noticed the table was full, with only one seat remaining open. Smack dab in between his cousin Charlie and the lady who haunted his every thought.

Selina sat with her head down, sipping from her cup. Conversations floated all around, but like always, no one directed any toward her. Duncan scowled at her forlorn expression. Even her own father ignored her. He glanced around the table for Lucas, but came up empty. Lucas wasn't at breakfast, and neither was Abigail. When his gaze landed on Charlie, she smirked at his predicament, then tilted her head at the empty seat, daring him to take it. What choice did he have?

"There he is. About time you joined us, my boy," Colebourne belted out, drawing everyone's attention toward Duncan. "Late night?"

Duncan nodded, sliding into the empty seat. "Aye."

"Your late night would have nothing to do with a missing bottle of my finest whiskey, would it?"

"Perhaps," Duncan mumbled.

"As I was saying, Norbury, the youth of today have no priorities," Colebourne scoffed.

Norbury nodded. "I agree. The very reason we have secured Gray and Selina's wedding date. Two less misguided souls floundering around without direction."

Selina stiffened next to Duncan at her father's statement. He stole a glance out of the corner of his eye, noticing her pinched expression. Her hands curled into fists in her lap.

"Exactly. Their union shall be an excellent statement of structure and priority for all to replicate. The children they produce will continue the powerful lineage of superiority," Colebourne declared.

"Oh, what delightful babies they will make," Lady Forrester gushed.

Colebourne chuckled. "Yes, they will be beauties. I cannot wait to bounce them on my knees. Right, Norbury?"

"Humph. I will no more bounce them on my knees than I did Selina. Children are not meant to be seen or heard. They serve only one purpose in life, and that is to lay the foundation for monetary gains for future generations."

Selina grew more distressed next to Duncan. Her hands twisted over and over in her lap. He raised his head to glare at Norbury, only to find Uncle Theo's gaze focused on him. His stare dared him to disagree with

Norbury. The longer the silence grew, the more his uncle's stare filled with disappointment.

Duncan cleared his throat. "I disagree, Your Grace. Every child is a treasure to be loved as the precious beings they are. Children need to be guided with a firm hand, but allowed the freedom to discover their true passion in life."

During his argument, Duncan slid his hand under the tablecloth to settle over Selina's. He rubbed his thumb over her knuckles, soothing her distress. A light gasp escaped her lips at the contact. He didn't dare glance her way. For if he did, he feared how he would react to her vulnerability. It already wrapped around her in a cloak of unhappiness. A covering he wanted to discard and replace with joyful memories, but alas, he wasn't the one for the task.

Norbury didn't look convinced. "'Tis why I find relief for securing Selina's future with Lord Gray, a responsible gentleman who takes his responsibilities seriously. Not carousing all hours of the night, inebriating himself with his uncle's spirits, and rising mid-morning. You would do well to follow in your cousin's footsteps, Lord Forrester."

Duncan raised a brow. "And where is the prodigal groom?"

Selina tried not to wince from Duncan's grasp. While he tried to comfort her, her father's comments only infuriated him. His gentle caress across her knuckles soothed her fragile nerves. However, now she needed to calm him. She slid a hand away and laid it over his hand, returning the favor. Soon his grip relaxed and stayed firmly clasped with hers.

Selina tried to keep her heart from reacting to Duncan's kind gesture. However, she failed. When the seating arrangement forced him to sit next to her, she had prepared herself for his snide remarks. She soon relaxed when he paid her no attention. But her father's arrogance alerted him to Selina's distress. When he offered her kindness, her heart gave a tug of awareness. Not only his kindness set her heart to race faster. Duncan's very nearness awakened every sense she tried to repress.

Shame overcame Selina at her father's comments. She'd suffered through his coldness and detachment her entire life. His declaration on how he regarded her and how her very existence was but a means to an end humiliated Selina. She wondered how her life would have differed if she'd had a caring parent, like Duncan described. She never knew her mother, and her father refused to talk about her. If her mother had lived, would her life have taken a different path? If she'd had a gentle hand to guide her, would her personality shine brighter?

Selina raised her head when the room remained silent. No one had yet to answer Duncan's question on Lucas's whereabouts. She had wondered where he was, but no one had engaged her in a conversation during the meal. At first, she hadn't realized he wasn't present. The overcrowded table flowed with conversation all around her. Then Duncan strolled in, distracting her from anyone else.

Lucas's cousins Charlotte and Evelyn were present with their husbands, Lord Sinclair and Lord Worthington. Their sister Jacqueline sat across from them, discussing Gemma's wedding from the day before. Lady Forrester kept a conversation flowing between Selina's father and Colebourne. Which left Selina sitting alone and forgotten. However, not only was Lucas missing, but Colebourne's ward, Abigail Cason, was missing too. Was it a coincidence?

"Where every responsible groom should be. He has traveled to your uncle's estate to prepare for the wedding. Perhaps, in his absence, you can step into his shoes and take care of his responsibilities. It is the least you can do to repay your uncle's hospitality," Norbury declared.

Duncan growled at the duke's audacity and was on the verge of declaring what the duke could do with his orders. However, Selina stopped him with a simple request.

"Please don't," she whispered.

Duncan snarled his displeasure, but he kept his opinion to himself. He wanted to rage at Norbury for how he treated his daughter. Then there was the matter of Lucas and his swift escape. Responsible. Humph. His cousin ran as fast and as far away from the situation as he could. To think Duncan gave him a promise to stand by his side. Well, his promise was now null and void.

While keeping a firm hold on Selina's hand, Duncan turned to Charlie. "Where is Abigail?" he whispered.

Charlie shook her head and mouthed, "Not now."

He narrowed his gaze, refusing to relent. "Where?" he growled.

Charlie sighed. "Colebourne Manor."

Selina gasped. Duncan closed his eyes, realizing she'd heard Charlie's answer. When she tried to pull her hands away, Duncan only tightened his grasp. He turned back to Selina and found the fiery temptress sitting proudly before them. While her face paled, her eyes lit with fury as she erected her walls once again. Over the last few weeks, she'd lowered them when Gemma befriended her. However, the rest of the family treated her no differently. Therefore, she raised her armor to protect herself again.

Duncan wished Selina would unleash her fury. He would even take it upon himself to bear the singes of her injustices. With Lucas's absence, his decision to stand back and allow their union ended at this moment.

Selina Pemberton was his.

And he would do everything in his power to make her so. Come a month's time, she wouldn't marry Lucas. Instead, Duncan would become her husband. He would make it his personal responsibility for Selina to experience nothing but happiness in her life. He knew he had a fight on his hands, but she deserved nothing less.

"Lady Forrester, I shall leave Selina in your care for the day. Colebourne, thank you for the meal, and I shall see you at your estate next week. Selina, please walk me out." Norbury laid his napkin on the table and disappeared without even waiting for Selina to accompany him.

Selina tugged her hands away and rose. "Excuse me," she murmured, following her father.

Duncan watched Selina walk away, wanting to follow. He started to rise when Charlie tugged his suit coat to remain seated. She nodded toward their uncle, who regarded him with a questioning stare. If he followed Selina, it would only draw unwanted attention in their direction. He would wait, and if she didn't return soon, he would make his excuses to find her.

Colebourne folded his hands and pointed his fingers at Duncan. "Norbury made a valid point where you are concerned."

Duncan huffed. "And that would be?"

"I will need you to escort your mother and Lady Selina around town for the day. I am afraid I cannot spare any servants to their care. They are otherwise engaged, preparing for our return to the country."

Duncan gritted his teeth. "If you insist."

Colebourne nodded. "I do."

Duncan never replied and started eating. His cousins talked among themselves, and their husbands debated the merits of the horseflesh they'd purchased at Tattersalls. He finished his meal, and Selina still hadn't returned. Duncan couldn't blame her.

He rose and pushed his chair back underneath the table. "If you will please excuse me. I have some matters to attend to before I escort you around town, Mother. Please send word when you are ready to leave."

"Yes, dear," Lady Forrester replied.

Duncan strode from the breakfast room, intending to find Selina before his family took their leave from the table. He only had a slim window of opportunity to catch her alone and planned to make the best of it. His path took him to the foyer. Hopefully, she was still engaged with her father. However, the footman informed him the Duke of Norbury had left immediately. When he questioned him on Selina's whereabouts, he pointed Duncan toward the library.

He pressed his ear against the door, listening for any bouts of crying. However, only silence met him. Perhaps the servants were wrong. He opened the door, closing it behind him after he stepped inside. Duncan glanced around the library and found Selina on a small step ladder, perusing the titles in the corner section. He strode to the ladder and glanced up, catching the sight of a very shapely calf. If he were to lean in closer, he would get a satisfying eyeful and a kick in his face. He stepped back to avoid any injury. In time, he would gaze on all her fleshy wonders.

"I would have never thought you held an interest in poetry."

Selina kept staring at the titles. "There is much you do not know of me."

"Ahh, but there is much I wish to learn of you," Duncan drawled, and his hand, having a mind of its own, brushed across her ankle.

Selina shook off his touch in annoyance. "Once again, sir, you take liberties I have not allowed."

Duncan smiled at her uptightness. "Mmm. My only excuse to plea is that I cannot resist such sweet temptation."

Selina faced the books and struggled to keep her breathing under control. His very nearness shook her composure. She'd stolen away into the library because she couldn't face another minute alone with Colebourne's family, especially after her father's arrogant tirade. She bit back the sigh from the caress of his fingers across her ankle. Selina snuck a peek below her to find Duncan staring up her dress. Her gaze lingered on his dark, tousled head leaning close as he brushed a whisper-soft kiss across her ankle. The searing heat from his lips seeped through her stocking, branding her.

Her foot kicked out in shock, and her slipper connected with his cheek, knocking him back. Selina gasped and rushed down the steps, only to find herself trapped. Duncan had reacted quicker than she had and grabbed a hold of the ladder rungs. She was unprepared to come so close to him. Her eyes widened at his devious smile, and she gulped.

Her hand lifted to his cheek, offering comfort. The redness glared at her in its fury. "I am so sorry."

"Are you not going to kiss it and soothe the sting?" he asked, pressing closer.

"Lord Forrester, I apologize. Allow me to call for a cold compress."

He reached for her hand and drew it to his lips, placing a kiss on her palm. His lips trailed to her wrist, softly nipping.

"Only a kiss will do," Duncan whispered.

Selina closed her eyes, fighting with herself. Her father's warning echoed in her head.

Walk the straight and narrow, Selina. Make sure your every action is within the proper guidelines. If this union does not occur, then it better hold no fault of yours. If it is, then I shall disown you. You will walk away with nothing. Do I make myself clear, daughter?

However, Duncan's whispers held more power over her. How much harm could come from one simple kiss? 'Twas as if they hadn't shared a kiss before. And the fault of his injury lay with her. She wanted to indulge in just one more kiss before she walked the line her father demanded of her.

Selina leaned forward and brushed her lips across Duncan's cheek. Once. Twice. Soft little kisses to ease his pain. Her fingers slid into his soft mane while her lips trailed across his smooth skin. She inhaled his cologne, his scent reminding her of the kisses he'd stolen from her lips. Forbidden kisses. Scandalous temptation. Everything she must resist, but wanted a taste of before she pledged herself to a lonely marriage. Her lips passed over his. Once. Twice. Soft little kisses to ease the ache suffocating her.

Duncan held his breath. He didn't dare move, for fear of breaking the fragile spell wrapping around them. He teased her, not believing she would actually kiss him. This was a side of Selina she'd never shown him before, a side she kept hidden. One he hoped she continued to display. When her lips trailed back to his and hovered over his lips, he moaned in the anticipation of her kiss.

His moan should have been a warning to stop this madness. However, the sound vibrated through her soul, soothing the jagged edges. When Duncan held her in his arms and kissed her, he made every second she spent alone worth it for a small amount of pleasure. His kisses made her forget her lonely existence and gave her memories to fantasize about, ones where she imagined someone loved her. Oh, she wasn't a silly fool who believed his kisses meant more than what they were. She was only a distraction for him to toil with during his boredom. He made it his mission to break her coldness, all for his amusement.

However, at this moment, she didn't care. After hearing her fiancé had left town to follow another lady and suffering his family's cold indifference at breakfast, Selina only wanted affection. Any sort of affection, no matter how insincere it might be. *Kiss me*, Selina wanted to whisper. When Duncan didn't answer her silent plea and remained unmoving, she took it upon herself to take what she wanted.

She stroked her tongue across his lips, teasing them open. They answered her silent command, and she slid her tongue inside to stroke across his. The only sign Duncan showed of his pleasure was the moans humming in his chest. It was enough of a sign for Selina to deepen the kiss. Her tongue skirted across his. When he responded, she retreated, exploring his mouth. Selina tasted the bitter flavor of the coffee he favored, with a hint of whiskey. Selina wondered why he'd turned to the bottle last night.

Was he haunted by their kiss in the chapel? Or by the threat he'd issued her? It was a useless threat, one he would never act upon, no matter how much Selina's heart begged for him to. As much as a scoundrel he was, Duncan was honorable above all else. He would never betray his family, especially for the likes of her.

As the desperation of Selina's thoughts grew, her kiss turned dark and possessive. The stroke of her tongue grew bolder, and her fingers dug into his hair, pulling his head closer.

Duncan suffered Selina's agony with every pull of her mouth against his. His mind and body were in tune with Selina, and he sensed when his dare turned into her desperate attempt to seek comfort from him.

Duncan ached to take possession of the kiss and prove how precious she was to him. She was somebody special. She was his. However, it wasn't his to control. This kiss was about her. For her to discover the strength she held to make her own decisions. For her to understand he was the key to her happiness. Her future. Her everything.

So she remained in control for now. After this kiss, all gloves were off. Duncan would be her groom and Selina his bride.

Selina pulled away from the drugging effect of Duncan's lips. When her moan mingled with his, she knew she needed to put an end to this madness. Nothing could become of their kiss, only scandal. Any moment now, Lady Forrester would search for her. If she were to find Selina in her son's arms, Selina would fall out of the lady's favor, a connection she had come to cherish. Between Gemma's friendship and Lady Forrester's kindheartedness, Selina had started feeling as if she belonged. If only in a small way.

"All better?" Selina's question came out huskier than she expected. She cleared her throat, avoiding Duncan's gaze.

Duncan inwardly groaned at the sexy hum of her voice. *No, my dear, my ache has only grown stronger.*

If she gifted him with a simple kiss for a harmless tap, how would she have responded to his more intimate thoughts? How would Selina ease the ache that had consumed him for months now? Ever since he first laid his lips upon her to distract her, he became lost and floundered, grasping at his sanity, only to fall deeper and deeper with unbidden thoughts of them sinking into a pleasure they both craved. He couldn't even bring himself to forget her engagement to another gentleman, even when he knew how unattainable she was. It never stopped him from hoping. Hope haunted him, tempting him into believing in the impossible. Well, no more.

He needed to stare into her eyes, but she avoided him. Her nervous glance skittered around the library, landing everywhere but on him. Duncan's smile widened. Oh, Selina. He would find much pleasure in the chase to come.

"Aye, lass. All better."

Selina swung her gaze to him, hearing the humor in his reply. She expected more of his torment to come. However, he only stepped back from the ladder and held out his hand to help her down. After her feet touched the floor, he lifted her hand and brushed a kiss across her knuckles. With a bow, he turned and left without a single taunt.

She sighed, leaning back against the rungs of the ladder. Selina pressed her knuckles against her cheek. The warmth of his lips remained. Or perhaps her imagination conjured more of the simple gesture than what it was.

The bittersweetness of their kiss was only a reminder of how her heart yearned for the wrong cousin.

Chapter Four

"If you will please excuse me, too. I must see to my packing. I am eager to return home," said Jacqueline.

"Of course, dear. Would you like to join me and Lady Selina on our shopping excursion?" asked Aunt Susanna.

Jacqueline smiled. "No, I shall decline. I hope you enjoy yourselves."

"Very well. Enjoy your day."

Colebourne waited for Jacqueline to say her goodbyes to her sisters. They made promises to visit before they returned to the estate. As he watched Jaqueline leave, she appeared melancholy. Now with Gemma wed and Abigail pleading for him to allow her to take a governess job in the Highlands before Lucas's wedding, she was all alone. He wished he could've seen her settled before he attempted his next matchmaking scheme.

However, Norbury threatened him with breaking the betrothal if Lucas and Selina didn't marry by the end of the year. Even though he had no intention of allowing Lucas and Selina to wed, Colebourne didn't want her father to promise her to another gentleman. He had noticed the attraction between Selina and his nephew at the house party he held before the season started. Colebourne decided then to make their match, but Duncan questioned his motives with his behavior as of late. His ill-treatment of

Selina made him wonder if he'd made the wrong decision. However, he'd changed his mind after Duncan's behavior at Gemma's wedding celebration.

Duncan couldn't keep his gaze off Selina the entire day, had even followed her back to the chapel during the reception. If Colebourne wasn't mistaken, they'd shared a kiss. Which led Duncan to drink his sorrows away. The closer the wedding drew, the more agitated Duncan grew. However, during breakfast this morning, he'd caught Duncan comforting Selina. Oh, not where anyone saw. However, it didn't go past him to notice Duncan holding Selina's hand underneath the table.

It had been foolish of him not to have seen the callous disregard Norbury treated Selina with. No wonder the poor girl lashed out. While Colebourne didn't condone her spiteful behavior, it made more sense why she behaved as she had. With a little extra guidance, Selina would display her true character. And to do so, he would require a little extra assistance on this match.

"Thank you for joining us for breakfast this morning," said Aunt Susanna.

Charlie laughed. "It was not as if we had much of a choice." She quirked an eyebrow at Colebourne. "Did we, Uncle Theo?"

Colebourne chuckled. "We all have choices, Charlie, my girl."

Sinclair and Worthington scoffed behind their napkins. Everyone in this room was aware of Colebourne's meaning behind his statement. Choices he controlled. But they wouldn't argue because, without his interference, their unions wouldn't have been possible. That and the old man would always take credit for their matches. And to please their wives, they continued with the farce.

Charlie rubbed her hands together. "So who is next?"

"Do you require our help with this match?" Evelyn's voice rose with excitement.

"Of course he does. Why else would he have demanded our presence this morning and waited until everyone left to approach the subject?" stated Charlie.

Evelyn gasped. "Is it Jaqueline? It must be. Why else wait until she left the room?"

"Which unsuspecting bloke do you plan to trap this time?" quipped Worthington.

Charlie narrowed her gaze at Worthington. "Trapped? Is that how you view your marriage to Evelyn?"

"Charlie," Sinclair and Evelyn warned.

"What? He is the one who used the word trap."

"You know very well our marriage is an enjoyment we feel blessed to live every day," Evelyn reprimanded.

Worthington leaned over to kiss Evelyn on the cheek and gazed into her eyes. "That is putting it mildly, my love." Then he whispered something into Evelyn's ear to make her blush.

"All right, all right. We get the picture, Lord Worthington," muttered Charlie.

The table chuckled over how even after Worthington proved his utter devotion toward Evelyn, Charlie was still overprotective of her twin.

Colebourne sighed. "As much as I wish Jaqueline was next, 'tis not her."

"Abigail then." Sinclair nodded. "We will help in any way possible. Worthington and I are acquainted with a few gentlemen from the club who will make an excellent match for Abigail."

"A kind offer, Sinclair, but 'tis not Abigail either."

Charlie started laughing uncontrollably. Everyone at the table stared at her in confusion, except for Uncle Theo and Aunt Susanna. They waited patiently for her to get herself under control. Tears leaked from her eyes, and she wiped them away before laughing harder.

"Seriously? How long have you known?" Charlie asked in between her bouts of laughter.

Colebourne nodded. "Since the house party. Various occurrences during the season confirmed my suspicions."

Charlie smiled in amusement. "Count me in. Oh, this will be so much fun. Neither one of them will realize they are your next victims."

"Who?" asked Evelyn.

"Duncan and Selina," Charlie announced before Uncle Theo could.

"Ohhh." Evelyn's eyes grew wide. Then she grimaced at Aunt Susanna. "Umm. Does this match set well with you?"

"Oh, yes. Selina is the perfect lady for Duncan," Aunt Susanna gushed. "The air sizzles when they are together."

"What is it you require of us?" asked Worthington.

Colebourne steepled his fingers together, gazing at them shrewdly. "I will need your assistance in keeping the Duke of Norbury occupied. He is proving himself more unbearable the closer we get to the impending wedding. His treatment of his own daughter is deplorable. Until they speak their nuptials, Norbury will keep his shrewd gaze focused on Selina. For Duncan to steal any moments alone with Selina, we must distract the duke."

"Does Forrester know of your matchmaking effort?" asked Sinclair.

Colebourne laughed. "He does not hold a clue."

"Then what makes you think he wishes to steal any time alone with Selina?" asked Evelyn.

Colebourne quirked a brow. "Where do you suppose he is now?"

"Oh, you are sneaky, Uncle Theo. You knew he would follow her." Charlie looked at Evelyn. "Why else do you think he told us where to sit this morning? He forced Duncan to sit next to Selina." Her gaze swung to her uncle. "Did you see him offering her comfort?"

"Yes, I did."

"I do not see how Charlie and I can be of any help. Norbury does not carry a high opinion of women and never speaks to us," said Evelyn.

Colebourne gazed at them seriously. "I need you girls to put your differences aside and befriend Selina. Her past behavior needs to be forgiven, and she needs to feel welcomed into our family. What I ask of you may seem unfavorable, but take a step back and see what life has been like for Selina. I am not justifying her past actions, but only asking for you to put yourself in her shoes. How would you have handled yourselves?"

"Will you require our presence before the wedding, then?" asked Evelyn.

"Yes. If you can, please come for an extended visit."

The two sisters stared at each other, reading each other's thoughts like they did. Then they each glanced at their husbands. Sinclair and Worthington both agreed with a nod.

"Worthington and I will follow you to Colebourne Manor," said Evelyn.

"Sinclair and I will visit every day," Charlie agreed too.

"Excellent. You gentlemen will keep Norbury distracted, and you ladies will find every opportunity for Lady Selina and Duncan to fall in each other's paths. When Lady Selina speaks her wedding vows, it will be to the gentleman who deserves her. And my son is not that gentleman." Colebourne raised his teacup to toast his plan.

Colebourne rested back in his chair while his nieces thought of instances to throw the couple together. Sometimes one needed to draw in extra recruits to make a plan a success.

What better help than the ones who understood the subjects so well?

Chapter Five

Forrester shifted in the small space he'd claimed for himself while waiting for Selina to finish her fitting. He listened to his mother gushing over the style and fit of her wedding gown. He itched to peek through the curtain for a glimpse. But the modiste's assistant kept trailing in and out of the dressing room, and it would draw too much attention toward him. So, he remained hidden in the dark corner. It was the perfect spot to hear and see all. Many mamas fussed over their debutante daughters, and many mistresses spent their lover's money foolishly.

He sighed when another hour passed and they were no more finished than when they had begun. His uncle thought to punish him with his demands, but they backfired on the old man. The demand gave him the opportunity to spend the day with the lady he most desired. Even his mother acting as a chaperone didn't hamper his enjoyment. His mother had promised this establishment was their last stop for the day. However, she never informed him of how long of an ordeal it would become. If she had, he would have at least grabbed a book to eliminate his boredom.

Forrester chuckled to himself, remembering Selina's reaction when he climbed into the carriage. She kept trying to avoid his stare throughout the afternoon. Her nervous replies to every question his mother asked amused him. Selina's apprehension increased with each stop they took, especially when his mother asked his opinion regarding Selina's trousseau.

One would think, with as much as he contributed, he was the groom. A slight matter he would change in the weeks to come. He only needed to formulate a plan on how to seduce his cousin's soon-to-be bride.

Soon, his mother walked out from behind the curtain with the modiste. The assistant followed them with a bundle of fabric in her arms. They walked farther into the shop, discussing the date for when the items needed delivered and the perfect finishing touches for the elegant garments. Forrester stood, expecting Selina to exit. He began to worry when each minute dragged into the next and she never departed.

He stepped out of the corner and peered into the shop, noting his mother talking to the assistant and the modiste helping a customer with a new bonnet. Once he realized no one paid him any attention, he took a peek behind the curtain. Forrester peeled the shade back slightly, expecting Selina had changed back into her day dress. However, the sight before him left him standing in awe.

Selina stood on a platform facing three mirrors. Each mirror angled to show the full impact of a gown worn by a customer. The mirrors staring back at Selina didn't do her a bit of justice. No, their reflection displayed a lady standing in an exquisite creation. However, he only saw a ravishing beauty who made the gown shine.

A soft pink gown fell over her creamy skin in waves and waves of exquisite silk. The demure neckline, while proper, would tease the groom with anticipation of their wedding night. The sleeves ended right above her elbow, with tiny jewels decorating the material. Long white gloves made of the finest silk and lace adorned her hands, sliding up her arm to meet where her sleeves ended. A white ribbon adorned her waist. An overwhelming desire rose in Forrester to wrap his hands around her hips and trace the path of the ribbon around her body.

While the front of her dress was demure, the back was an invitation to sin. The dress dipped low, exposing her back. It teased a man to stroke his hand along her curves to see if her skin was as smooth as the material of her gown. A long pearl necklace clung to her neck, dropping along her back.

When they left the townhome, Selina's hair had been styled in a bun and hidden under a bonnet. Now her long blonde tresses were loose and gathered together with a strand of pearls and laid across one shoulder.

Obviously, she hadn't noticed him yet because she stood there, swishing her dress back and forth and humming to herself. Forrester was on the verge of dropping to his knees and begging Selina to run away with him. Her carefreeness wiped away her vulnerability, and she appeared at peace. But most of all, she appeared happy. Which left him in doubt of his pursuit. Did she want to marry Lucas? Did he fool himself into believing she was better off with him?

Forrester hadn't realized his steps took him to her side until she gasped his name, her aqua-colored eyes meeting his in the mirror.

"You are an achingly magnificent sin I wish to indulge in," Forrester's raspy voice whispered around them.

"You must leave," Selina whispered in return, never once breaking his gaze.

Duncan shook his head at her order. The desire in his eyes rocked her core. The air sizzled around them, sucking her deeper into the fantasy she'd created of a universe where only the two of them existed. Their connection was more intense than any moment they'd shared before. The kiss they shared earlier held nothing on the ache consuming her now. If he didn't kiss her, Selina would perish from sheer need alone.

His hand reached out to touch her gown, caressing the smooth fabric. Selina repressed a groan, wishing he'd touch her instead. Duncan didn't make her wait, but slid his hand under the gown and his rough fingers stroked up her leg. Slowly, so achingly slow. She closed her eyes from the sensations. Her knees trembled.

Oh, she was softer than the silk. His hand traveled higher, his fingers sinking into her thigh. He tormented himself, sliding them higher. Selina's heat tempted him to touch her. To stroke a sigh from her lips. To weaken her legs so she would fall into his arms. As his hand moved higher, her eyes opened, and he watched them change color. The cool aqua soon turned to a turbulent turquoise, revealing her every desire. As much as Selina denied him, she craved him with a need so uncontrollable, she wouldn't know how to handle the emotions their union would cause. He would soon show her.

But not now. With much reluctance, he drew his hand away.

Selina groaned when he released his hand, her body betraying her need. She must reprimand him and order him to leave. However, she only craved for him to kiss her. The desire consuming her wanted him to do the wicked things his touch ignited. His closeness only intensified her need.

He slowly circled her, taking in every detail of her dress, his stare stroking the flames higher. If one could melt from a stare alone, Selina felt herself doing so. When he walked around her the second time, his fingers left a trail of tiny sparks in its wake. They traveled back and forth across the fabric above her bosom, then trailed along her shoulder and down her arm, ending at her elbow. His fingers traced over the jeweled decorations. As she watched the spellbinding act, her nipples tightened.

She wondered if he would caress her in the same manner. Would his touch be tender? Or would it hold the power of his need? Duncan walked behind her, and she gasped when he trailed his hand down her back, his hand dipping under the pearls, stroking up and down. She caught his gaze in the mirror when he bent his head to kiss her neck. His eyes spoke volumes of his admiration.

Selina tipped her head to rest on his shoulder while he placed a path of kisses along her neck. His doubts on pursuing her vanished at her response from his simple caress. She trembled in his arms with her body's desire. Duncan noticed her nipples tighten when he traced the jewels on the dress. His smile turned wicked, imagining what they would taste like. Sweet, but sinful. A decadent dessert.

His lips trailed to her ear and sucked her earlobe between his teeth. Then back down to her shoulder. He paused, waiting. His hands dropped to her hips and held her still before circling around to her stomach. He slid them up her chest, brushing across the tight buds. Duncan ached to kiss the gasp from her lips, but once he began, there was no way in hell he would stop. He wouldn't gain her by a scandal—only by seduction alone.

Her gaze flew to his, and he kissed her shoulder one last time. "A sin I will find much pleasure from. After you say I do, I promise I will make love to you while you wear this gown."

Selina moaned. "Duncan."

"You, my love, are a vision."

Selina ached for Duncan to kiss her, his promise lost in the sensation of his touch. With one more lingering caress, he walked away from her with his usual confident swagger. He left Selina trembling with an unfilled ache and begging for more. While she stood searching for any sign that he wasn't toying with her emotions. Anything.

"Duncan," Selina whispered.

Duncan paused at her whisper. He hung his head, and Selina noticed his hands fight for control. They curled and uncurled into fists. Selina heard his deep sigh from where she stood. She silently begged him to turn around. Each second passed in agonizing slowness. Then, before he left, he turned. It was then Selina received her sign. His gaze held a look of unbreakable determination.

Which left Selina wondering. Did she hold the power to resist him? And did she even want to?

Chapter Six

She walked inside Colebourne Manor for the last time as Selina Pemberton. From this day forth, it would become her home. A home where she never felt comfortable. The next few weeks would gauge her future as Gray's wife. Colebourne was slowly marrying his wards off. Only Jacqueline and Abigail remained. At times, the manor would fill with the visiting families, but Selina could endure those brief visits.

However, she didn't know how she would handle living under the same roof as the woman her fiancé loved.

She'd be a fool not to notice the longing glances shared between Gray and Abigail. They always found a way to gravitate toward each other. Their close relationship was the very reason Selina had lashed out with her vindictiveness over the years. Throughout her life, her father told Selina that Lucas Gray was hers. In her younger years, she had fooled herself into believing that since they were to wed, then they must love each other too. But as she grew older, she realized love didn't occur because of a promised agreement. It happened when two souls connected and merged into one. That was not Selina and Gray.

Every minute spent in his company, he treated her with politeness, but nothing else. Never once had he regarded her with affection. No soft touches. No stolen kisses. No passion. Nothing but tolerance. Each day that drew them closer to their wedding, his tolerance unraveled more and more.

His polite attitude turned curt and couldn't even be described as nice. His stand on their marriage was more than clear.

To make matters worse, Gray's distraction drew her father's attention. The entire carriage ride from London, her father had lectured Selina on how important it was to secure Lucas Gray as her husband. He'd made his point clear. Either she married Gray or she would find herself abandoned in one of his holdings for the rest of her life. She would no longer have the access to any coin or lovely gowns. No more freedom. She would live a simple existence.

He'd tried to threaten her with how lonely her life would be if she didn't become Lady Gray. However, it wasn't a threat to Selina. Only a blessing. She wouldn't have to pretend interest in charming a gentleman who didn't even care for her, or please her father anymore. The solitude wouldn't bother her either because it was how she existed now and would if she married Gray. So her father's threats didn't scare her. If anything, the relief gave her hope for what her future might hold.

After Duncan caressed her in the dress shop, it had made her dream of a different outcome. She didn't want to marry Lucas Gray, but she would if he didn't break off the betrothal. Gray would only break free once he realized the depth of his feelings for Abigail. Selina wanted to help bring them together. It was the least she could do after her years of terror toward the young miss.

Jealousy. It made one react in a vengeful manner. She remembered every snide remark she'd made over the years. Since she'd gained insight into her emotions, remorse settled in. To redeem herself, she would need to befriend Lucas's family and bite her tongue at every sarcastic remark. If they spoke harshly toward her, then she would refrain from lashing out with her own spiteful comments. It would take every ounce of patience she had.

Selina held faith in accomplishing a change in her behavior. The carriage ride with her father proved how determined she was. She answered every comment with a "yes, sir" to pacify him. Even when she didn't agree with his views.

As for the matter of Duncan Forrester, she still had no clue. Her heart urged her to explore his stolen kisses. To embrace his soft caresses. To open herself to his love. However, she still wasn't sure if it was love. She argued with herself that Duncan only lusted after her. Maybe he found the allure of the sinful temptation dangerous and exciting.

Over the years, he had shown no kindness toward her. He always ignited her temper and toyed with her emotions. Now it appeared as a game he played to drive a wedge between her and Gray. If Selina's thoughts were sensible, she would see the simple reason for Duncan's behavior. Duncan, like the rest of Gray's family, wanted her out of the picture so Gray could pursue Abigail.

Duncan toyed with her to lead her astray. He sacrificed himself for Gray's happiness. Also, it was what Duncan did best. He was a scoundrel who chased one skirt after another. Leaping from one torrid affair into the next, with not a care except for his own satisfaction. If he chased her, it might cause a rift in his family's dynamic, but he would come out like a knight in shining armor, while Selina's reputation would hang in tatters with ridicule. She would become shunned and labeled a whore, leaving her family forever in disgrace just because she couldn't control her own lustful cravings.

She needed to harden her heart to resist Duncan Forrester until she brought Gray and Abigail together or failed with her own walk down the aisle to Gray. If she succeeded and Duncan still showed interest, then she would open her heart to him. If Duncan didn't continue with his interest, then it proved she was only an amusement to him.

~~~~~~

Duncan watched Selina from his spot at the top of the staircase. He lounged against the railing, observing her actions. She walked around the foyer, gently touching picture frames on the wall and picking up the objects on the tables before sitting them back down again. He frowned at her forlorn expression. *What consumes her thoughts?* Did she picture herself as duchess of the manor? Or had his kiss struck doubt in her mind?

No matter her thoughts, it didn't take away from her beauty. After a lengthy carriage ride from London, her appearance looked fresh, with nothing out of place. Her gown was more elaborate than what his cousins wore in the country, and it only highlighted her beauty. When she arrived, she had followed her father inside and tried to stay invisible, wincing at his demands toward Colebourne's staff. If one wondered how she acquired her sharp tongue, they only needed to observe her father in action. Duncan's mother had soothed Norbury, ushering him away to Uncle Theo's study, leaving Selina alone.

Selina undid her bonnet, slipping it from her head. A few stray curls fell from her bun. He ached to curl them around his fingers, caressing the softness while placing a soft kiss against her neck. He could hear her sighs now. Duncan chuckled. She wouldn't sigh, but rail at him instead. It would mortify Selina if he attempted to touch her where anyone might come upon them. It was a risk he was willing to take for any reaction but the sadness surrounding her.

He pushed away from the railing, on his way to tease Selina, when Charlie stopped him with a sarcastic comment.

"Is the dragon inspecting her new lair? I imagine she is taking stock of the family's holdings," Charlie quipped.

He turned his head to glare at his cousin.

Charlie chuckled in amusement. "Ahh, still acting the protector, are ye? What are your intentions with the lass?" Charlie tried to tease a reaction from Duncan.

He shook his head at her poor attempt. "What are you doing here?"

"I came to visit Jacqueline, and I need to talk to you."

"Can it wait?" Duncan glanced to make sure Selina was still below. "No."

Selina walked down the corridor, out of his view. Duncan started down the stairs. "It must."

"Duncan," Charlie hissed. "'Tis important I speak with you."

Duncan paused, sighing. "Same time? Same place?"

"It will have to do. I will have to endure Jasper's fury. 'Tis too important not to tell you."

Duncan nodded, running down the stairs. He followed the direction where Selina headed, his stride quickening with each step. He took a peek into each room, searching for her. His steps slowed when he found her pressing her ear against the door to his uncle's study. Her brows were drawn together, and the frown from earlier pinched her lips.

Duncan leaned against the wall, whispering, "You will fit in quite nicely with this family."

Selina gasped, stepping away from the door. "I do not know what you speak of. I was knocking on the door for permission to enter." She wiped her hands down her skirt.

Duncan smirked. "With your ear?"

Selina glared at him, refusing to answer.

"If you would grant me a smile, perhaps I might show you a better spot for your eavesdropping. The door is too thick to hear anything worthwhile."

Selina narrowed her gaze, trying to decide if she could trust Duncan. She'd overheard her name mentioned in the room before they closed the doors and wanted to listen to what they discussed. Gray had joined her father and his for a discussion.

"Very well."

Duncan stayed leaning against the wall. She had yet to grant him a smile, and until she did, he wasn't moving. However, she remained stubborn, expecting him to give in.

"Well?"

"I made you an offer. I am waiting for you to fulfill your part of the bargain. Then I will fill mine."

Selina crossed her arms over her chest. "Now why would I fulfill my side when I am unsure if you will fulfill yours?"

"I call it trust, my love."

"I am not your love. Please stop referring to me as such."

"Oh, but you are." Duncan grabbed at her hand and held it over his heart. "Feel how it beats for you now."

Selina tried to pull her hand away, but Duncan kept it clasped in his. She glanced around to see if they were alone. Her knees weakened from the warmth of his touch. She bit her bottom lip when she felt his heart race against her palm. It wasn't a steady beat of his usual arrogance, but it hammered against his chest as hers did now. She raised her head and become trapped in his sensual gaze.

His other hand reached up to cup her cheek, his thumb brushing across her bottom lip. Back and forth, easing the tension. Her tongue accidentally brushed across his thumb, inciting a moan from Duncan. When he closed the gap between them, she closed her eyes, anticipating a kiss, one Selina had dreamed of since he'd admired her in her wedding gown.

Duncan wanted to groan at the picture before him. An innocent temptress silently begging for a kiss. A kiss he was but one step away from indulging in, scandal be damned. He bent his head to capture her luscious lips under his. To explore their sweetness and savor every delicious essence of Selina. She was worth the risk.

"There you are, dear." Lady Forrester's voice echoed along the hallway, jolting Selina from Duncan's hold.

As Selina's eyes widened in panic, Duncan looked up to the ceiling, cursing the heavens for his mother's interruption. He glanced over his shoulder to see his mother at the other end of the hallway, far enough away where she wouldn't have noticed their intimate embrace. However, Selina thought she had. He stepped farther away from her, putting a respectable amount of distance between them.

He turned toward his mother with an excuse on the tip of his tongue to pacify her when he noticed Charlie trailing behind, wearing a smirk of amusement. That minx. Since she aimed to sabotage his time with Selina, he withdrew his courtesy of meeting her later to talk. Only, he wouldn't inform her of not meeting her; instead, he would dangle enough information in Sinclair's ear of his wife's request for a late-night rendezvous. Yes, how glorious revenge was. Sinclair would become furious once he learned of Charlie agreeing to meet him later. Then he would see if Charlie ever interrupted him again in his pursuit of Selina Pemberton.

Selina blushed when Lady Forrester came upon them. "I was only … That is, Lord Forrester …" she stuttered.

"What Lady Selina is trying to say is that I offered to escort her to her father. She couldn't find him, and I told her of how I saw him going into Uncle Theo's study," Duncan explained.

Charlie snickered. "How gallant of you."

"Yes, it was. But then I raised him to be a gentleman, young lady." Lady Forrester shot Charlie a shrewd gaze.

"And a fine gentleman he is," Charlie continued with her teasing.

Duncan bowed before the ladies. "If you will excuse me, I promised to meet Sinclair in the stables." He gave Charlie a sinister grin. But she only shrugged her indifference.

"Thank you, Lord Forrester, for your assistance," said Lady Selina.

"My pleasure. Anytime I may help you, please do not hesitate to ask." He winked before he strolled away.

Selina felt warm from his intense stare and the wink he bestowed upon her. She knew her face had turned bright red from his brazen attention. She could only imagine what the ladies thought of their time alone. Perhaps she shouldn't have stared after him for so long. It would only cause them to wonder if they dallied with each other. Charlie wouldn't believe it possible. However, Lady Forrester would because, in Selina's distress a few weeks ago, she had confessed to Duncan's mother of the kiss they'd shared at the Kanfold Ball.

She raised her gaze and found them staring at her. One with amusement, the other with kind regard. Of course, Charlie found enjoyment any time Selina was uncomfortable. Lady Forrester only smiled with kindness, but Selina noted a devious sparkle in the lady's eyes.

Before she could discover the reason, Lady Forrester led her from the study door. "Please forgive me for abandoning you on your arrival. Your father was, well, I think over tired from the trip from London. I wanted to get him settled."

Selina patted the lady's hand. "No need to fret. I understand my father's habits. I apologize for his rudeness upon our arrival."

Lady Forrester led Selina upstairs to the bedchamber she would use before the wedding. She glanced over her shoulder to note Charlie following them at a discreet distance with a shrewd look upon her face. Selina gulped. She wanted to avoid any conflict with Gray's family, but it was impossible. Selina turned at the landing toward the bedchamber she'd used in her visits in the past. It was the wing dedicated to guests. The other wing was comprised of rooms for family members. However, Lady Forrester tugged on her arm to walk in the other direction.

"Am I not to have my regular bedchamber?"

Lady Forrester smiled. "No, my dear. In a few weeks, you will become a member of our family. 'Tis only fitting you have a bedchamber in the family wing."

"But will they not be in usage by the family members already?"

"For the most part. However, Gemma wanted to gift you with the usage of her bedroom," Lady Forrester explained.

"That was very kind of her." Selina looked around the room, noticing the elegance of Gemma's style.

The bedroom was painted a soft shade of pink with ivy etched around the windows. A white desk sat near the window next to a light blue chaise. On the nightstand stood a stack of books. Selina trailed her fingers over the titles. They were poems of her favorite poets. Next to them stood a vase full of wildflowers. A soft smile lit Selina's face.

It warmed her heart that Gemma still considered her a friend. She hadn't heard from her since Gemma married Lord Ralston. They had taken off on a honeymoon to visit Italy. She didn't expect to hear from her during this time, but it still hadn't stopped the doubts from entering Selina's mind that their friendship was only a figment of her imagination playing tricks on her. She only wished the other members of Gray's family would befriend her too. But those were wishful musings, and she couldn't fault them for not forgiving her. Selina had been the one to cause the animosity between them. As she moved forward, she planned to establish a foundation of kindness and generosity. If they didn't respond to the change in her character, then the fault no longer lay with her.

"I will let you get settled, and I shall see you at dinner." Lady Forrester turned at the door. "Oh, I almost forgot. Gemma sent you a note, and I laid it on top of the desk for you."

Selina smiled. "Thank you."

Lady Forrester glided out of the room, onto the next item needing taken care of for the household. She was a whirlwind Selina found hard to keep up with. Also, she was one of the most kindhearted ladies Selina knew. She had grown close to the lady over the last month planning her wedding. Her unwavering guidance gave Selina the confidence to change her personality for the better. She didn't want Lady Forrester to ever feel ashamed of her.

"So, you and Duncan?" Charlie startled Selina from her musings.

Selina swung her gaze to Charlie. "Excuse me?"

Charlie tilted her head, studying Selina. Selina grew nervous, wondering if Charlie had seen her and Duncan's intimate embrace. She must think of an explanation for why Duncan had pressed himself against her.

"Do you care for him?"

"I think you misunderstood what you witnessed. I tripped, and Lord Forrester only saved me from falling onto my face." Selina walked toward the desk.

Charlie watched Selina move items around on the desk. She avoided eye contact with her. Instead, Selina's gaze wandered around the bedroom, bouncing around, never staying still for a second. It was the same reaction Selina had when they had interrupted her and Duncan in the hallway outside of Uncle Theo's study.

Charlie had a choice to make. She could continue with her hatred for the lady before her. Or she could rise above Selina's behavior in the past and see her for the lady she had become from the gentle influence of Gemma, Aunt Susanna, and Uncle Theo. Charlie had noticed the changes in Selina's character and realized it was due to love. When Uncle Theo asked Charlie for her help, she had agreed because she wanted revenge against the dragon who tormented her family and knew she would find humor in toying with Duncan.

Charlie realized it was wrong if she continued with her act of vengeance. She owed it to the members of her family to help bring Selina and Duncan together. She'd seen for herself the love shining from Duncan's eyes when he stared at Selina before walking away. A tremendous amount of guilt lay on Duncan's shoulders. If he pursued his love, then he risked losing his family—even though his family secretly worked to help secure that love. She would have her fun of tormenting the two into a union, instead of tormenting Selina for revenge.

Charlie shook her head. "No. I did not misunderstand the affection passing between you two. Duncan almost kissed you, and you waited with anticipation."

Selina twisted her hands together. "No, no. Duncan only …" Selina realized her mistake by saying his Christian name.

Charlie smiled smugly. "You do care for him."

This time, it wasn't a question, but a statement. Selina couldn't deny it without opening another field of questions she didn't trust herself to answer. Also, she didn't trust Charlie the way she trusted Gemma. Charlie had always acted out vindictively when Selina was cruel toward the family. Would Charlie see Selina's feelings toward Duncan as an act of betrayal toward Lucas? Or would she sympathize with Selina? Perhaps even help her decide the right course of action.

Either way, she couldn't risk anyone else discovering the love she held for Duncan. For now, Selina would keep her feelings a secret.

Selina hardened her voice. "Does your family always engage in speaking nonsense?"

Charlie laughed, not intimidated one bit by Selina's surliness. It only proved Selina's fear in anyone discovering her most intimate secrets. Now Charlie understood why Selina reacted as she did when cornered. Gemma had been correct in befriending Selina, whereas the rest of them had failed and continued to fail. It was all a defense mechanism to protect her unloved heart.

"Welcome to the family, Selina," Charlie drawled, walking out of the bedchamber.

Selina didn't know what to make of Charlie's behavior, though she feared Charlie had read more into Duncan's flirting with her and come to the conclusion of Selina harboring feelings for him. Charlie was too persistent. Would she make it known how Selina cared for Duncan? Colebourne would break the betrothal, and Selina would find herself involved in the greatest scandal in the ton's history.

No, she must stay clear of Duncan and only allow herself time with him in the company of others. It shouldn't be too difficult. After all, this was a vast estate, and no one ever paid her any attention before.

Why should this visit be any different?

Chapter Seven

Somehow Selina had managed to stay away from Duncan for the past three days.

There were many close calls where he almost trapped her, but she slipped through his grasp. Even as early as this morning after they ate breakfast, he stopped her in the hallway and requested a walk around the garden. Thankfully, Gray had strolled by and grabbed Duncan for a ride. Selina should have felt annoyed at Gray for ignoring her, but she'd felt relief when he persuaded his cousin away.

She decided to walk through the garden by herself though. It was an excellent idea, after all. The perfect spot to reflect on the past few days. She filled her days with wedding plans and learning the responsibilities of her new title once she married Gray. Yet, she still suffered from loneliness. Colebourne's family regarded her with a polite indifference, their attitude remaining unfriendly.

This morning proved how unwelcome they were to Selina. Since Gemma so generously offered Selina her bedchamber, she'd encountered someone every time she went to her room. Not once did any of the ladies offer her an invitation to their early morning ritual. The first couple of days, it had only been Jacqueline and Abigail. However, yesterday, Evelyn and her husband, Lord Worthington, had arrived to stay until the wedding.

Now, with Evelyn visiting, Charlie arrived this morning for breakfast. Selina had listened to their laughter in the room across the hall, fighting not to allow envy to rule her actions. Once she fought against her vengeful pride, she walked by the room and didn't make one comment. The room had grown silent when she passed by, and they'd extended no offer for her to join them. She tried to keep the sadness from creeping in, but each rejection she endured unraveled her emotions further.

Duncan's offer for a walk around the gardens had lifted her spirits until she reminded herself how inappropriate it was for them to spend any time alone. Because she knew in her heart, the walk might appear innocent, but Duncan would turn it very indecent. As much as Selina's body craved his scandalous touch, she must resist him. So she couldn't find fault with Gray's treatment when, in the end, he saved her from throwing away her future on a simple infatuation that would lead nowhere but a lifetime of heartache.

Which left Selina only able to seek the company of her father for companionship. Except her father was another gentleman she wished to avoid. Because his company only consisted of more lectures. He analyzed her every move and commented on how she could improve herself. Her every action displeased him. Colebourne's encouragement was the only shining light that helped Selina survive this torturous affair.

Selina sighed, sitting on a bench. She watched the birds fly toward the fountain to take a sip before flying away. She closed her eyes, soaking in the sun's warmth to soothe her weary soul. Was she cut out for a life married to Gray and his coldhearted family? Or should she dip her toes into the temptation Duncan offered? She could indulge in an affair until her wedding day and then atone for her sins once she married Gray. Every glance from Duncan drew her closer to sinning, no longer caring who she might hurt in the affair. No one seemed to care about her feelings, so why did she for theirs?

Her conscience kept wrestling with her doubts. It was as if an angel sat on one shoulder, whispering in her ear to show patience and walk the path of goodness. On the other shoulder, the devil sat, grinning mischievously and urging to give in to her cravings and walk a path full of naughty twists and turns. Any time she ever caved into the devil's taunts, it only brought her misery. But she experienced the same misery, if not worse, as she walked down the angel's path now. So why bother? She wished she had a friend to confide in and for them to help guide her toward the best decision.

Selina pulled out Gemma's letter from her pocket. This was the closest connection to what she needed. She had read the letter multiple times since opening it. It gave her guidance on making the right decision. Selina needed Gemma's kind words and inspiration now more than ever.

Dear Selina,

I wish I could join you in your time of need. I will arrive shortly. For now, I offer you the usage of my bedchamber before your marriage to Lucas. I hope you find comfort in the room whenever your time becomes too daunting. Please show my family patience with their behavior toward you. It will take a while to overcome the actions from your past. But I believe in the magic of forgiveness.

Before your wedding day approaches, I plead for you to delve into your soul on the path that will make you whole. During this time, you have the chance to discover the depth of your emotions for D. versus the emotionless existence you feel with Lucas. Believe me when I say having your heart full of love and knowing the person you pledge your life to loves you in the same manner brings you a happiness you never knew existed. And I believe you can share this same happiness with D. And I am not pleading for you to throw Lucas over so Abigail has a chance with him. No, I am saying this as your friend. You deserve a happily ever after. Give D. a chance. Even if only for the selfish reason to feel loved for a short while.

Now that I have given you my friendly advice, I will conclude with a promise that I shall join you soon. After you make your decision on how to proceed, I will be there to hold your hand or offer my shoulder for you to cry upon. As you were there for my wedding to Barrett, I shall be there for yours.

Your loving friend,

Gemma

Selina sighed again. Could she act with selfish intentions and indulge in a scandalous affair with Duncan, if only for a short period before she married Gray? She still didn't understand the attraction she felt toward the man. He infuriated her more than anything. Except lately, he'd shown kindness to her, which only confused her more. Did he pity her? Even when he ignited her temper, a spark of desire lighted in her soul, awakening her emotions.

"That is a heavy sigh, lass."

The heavy Scottish brogue startled Selina. She quickly refolded Gemma's letter and slid it back inside her pocket. An older gentleman stood before her, wearing a kilt. His clothing appeared weathered, as did his face, telling Selina the man spent most of his time outdoors. His warm smile welcomed her to divulge her greatest secrets.

"I am trying to decide on how to handle a dilemma I am facing." Selina returned his smile.

"A difficult one?"

"Yes."

The old man glanced up to the sky and then around the garden. "A mighty fine day to make a life-altering decision."

Selina's forehead wrinkled. "Why do you say it is a life-altering decision? Perhaps 'tis only a small matter needing my attention."

"Ah, but any decision ye make in life will alter an outcome."

Selina laughed for the first time in days. "You have a point."

He winked. "I usually do."

Selina's smile kept growing wider. "Would you like to take a seat? I would love to hear more of your wise points."

"I would love to. However, I have spent the better part of the last week riding in a carriage, and I am in dire need to stretch these old limbs."

"From Scotland?"

"Aye."

"I do not mean to pry, but did you travel with a Forrester?"

The old man looked at Selina keenly. "Aye." His answer held no clue on who he might be.

Selina should introduce herself in a polite manner. However, her reputation preceded itself, and she didn't want to diminish the charm he extended toward her. Anyone who traveled with a Forrester would hold knowledge of her and probably not think too kindly of her or her father.

"Did you have a pleasant journey?" she asked instead.

"Aye, I did. The weather was pleasant, and the meals from the village inns were splendid."

"Can I tell you a secret?" she whispered.

The old man wandered closer to stand a couple of steps away and leaned forward with a curious smile on his face.

"I love the food from the inns. They hold so much more flavor in them. My father always grumbles about the fare, but I love it. I believe the atmosphere helps how I enjoy the food. There is no pretentious air of proper behavior, only the welcoming of being oneself."

"Exactly. I could not have voiced it better myself." He chuckled.

"Do you promise not to inform a soul?"

He reached out and patted her hand. "Your secret is safe with me, lass."

From there, they continued a light conversation, neither one of them offering to tell the other who they were. Selina decided he must be a servant from the state of his worn clothing and his simple philosophy of life. He didn't act superior, as most men of a higher station would. Nor did she act as her father would expect her to. He was a welcome burst of fresh air to her soul.

"I must leave you now. I have things I must see to. Thank you for the warm welcome. I have enjoyed our talk tremendously, and I hope to share more with you in the future."

Selina rose and smiled. "I look forward to it. Welcome to Colebourne Manor. I hope you enjoy your stay."

He nodded. "I shall. Good day, my lady."

"Thank you," answered Selina before he walked away.

He quirked an eyebrow. "Whatever for?"

Selina only shook her head.

He smiled kindly at her. "You are more than welcome then."

Selina watched him walk away and sat back down. She pondered the point he'd made and wondered, if she pursued her own happiness, could she alter the outcome for all the parties involved?

"Should I allow him to tempt me into the sin of immoral pleasures?" Selina murmured.

"Talking to oneself is a sure sign of madness," Duncan whispered near her ear.

Selina gasped, jumping off the bench. She whirled around with her hand pressed against her chest. "You frightened me. How long have you been standing there?"

"Long enough to admire your beauty, but too far away to hear your words."

"Then you did not hear what I …"

Duncan shook his head. "No, but I can tell by your blush that I missed out on hearing your shocking thoughts."

Selina brought her hands up to her cheeks to cool them off. "Nonsense. I only asked myself a question about what I should wear for dinner."

Duncan perused her up and down. "You look perfect to me. There is no need to change your dress. We are an informal bunch while in the country."

"Yes, I suppose you are correct."

Duncan winked. "I usually am."

Selina's brows wrinkled, a sense of déjà vu overcoming her. Duncan's response matched the other gentleman's comment. She shook her head. Coincidence, 'tis all. After all, the servant traveled with a Forrester, and Duncan was friendly with every soul he ever came into contact with. A perfect explanation was that Duncan had picked up the habit from the servant.

Selina turned to walk away. She hadn't made a decision yet, and if she spent even one more second with Duncan, she would cave.

"Selina, my love?"

She gritted her teeth before turning around. "I am not your love. Please stop spouting such nonsense before someone overhears," she hissed.

Duncan jumped over the bench, settled on the seat, and patted his lap. "Come join me for a spell. I wanted to spend time with you today in the garden, but Lucas dragged me away. You were going to answer yes earlier."

"Your thoughts are wrong."

"Ah, my love, do not be so cruel."

Selina stalked over to Duncan and stopped before him with her hands on her hips. "Stop this madness and leave me alone. I am to wed your cousin at the end of the month."

Duncan reached out and pulled her hands off her hips, coaxing her fists to open. When they did, he linked their fingers together. "But you have not wed him yet. I still have time to convince you otherwise."

"I must. 'Tis expected of me," Selina whispered.

Duncan tugged her forward. Selina lost her balance and landed in his lap, where he wrapped his arms around her and drew her close. She pressed her hand on his chest, trying to pull away, but Duncan only tightened his embrace.

"You do not have to do anything you do not want to do."

He lowered his head to draw Selina's lips into a gentle kiss, coaxing her to surrender to the passion that simmered under the surface whenever she was near. Each day, his desire grew stronger to make her his. He wanted Selina more than he'd ever wanted another soul. He wanted her softness, but most of all he wanted her fire.

His kiss deepened, drawing out her soft moans. Duncan slid his tongue across her lips. When she opened her mouth, his tongue swept in and danced alongside hers. Each stroke begged her to surrender to him. One of his arms kept Selina clasped against his chest, while his other arm swept along her curves, molding her to him.

"You have no desire to marry Lucas," he stated, catching his breath before kissing her again. "Lucas's kisses do not breathe life into your soul as mine do."

Selina moaned from the pleasure of Duncan's kiss. "Lucas has never kissed me."

Duncan wanted to beat his fists against his chest at her confession. If Lucas had never kissed her, then no other gentleman had either. She'd only gifted him with this affection. And no other would enjoy the privilege.

Duncan slid his hand under her skirt, caressing the length of her silken limbs. His touch traveled higher between the softness of her thighs. Her warmth beckoned his touch closer. "He is but a fool who shall never savor the sweetness he missed out on from your delectable lips." His kiss grew bolder as his hand brushed across her curls. Her groan was his undoing. "Then I can safely assume he has never held the pleasure of touching you either, has he?" Duncan asked as his fingers sank into her wetness.

They glided over her folds, drawing forth her breathy moans. Each moan heightened the pleasure of holding Selina in his arms. He slowly slid a finger inside her core, and her gasp sent a fresh ache to his cock. He grew harder at every sensation passing between them. As he soothed the ache consuming Selina, he watched her through heavy eyelids. She threw her head back, her eyes closed and her mouth parted open, allowing the heavenly sounds to surround them. Her cheeks glowed with a warm blush.

For the first time, Selina embraced their connection.

His stroke grew bolder as his thumb caressed her clit. Selina's fingers dug into his arms the closer her body reached the pinnacle of her desire. Duncan needed her to shatter in his arms. He needed to grab her soul and keep it captive until she surrendered to the passion they would create when they came together. He needed her love to make him whole.

Every rule ingrained in the strict structure of Selina's life whispered away in the wind whenever Duncan touched her. Even now, with the threat of being discovered, Selina was powerless to his seduction. For the first time, she closed off her thoughts of proper decorum and dived into the wanton depths of sin. Her body ached with a need only Duncan could fulfill. His very actions should have scandalized her, and she should have berated him. However, her heart fought against her common sense and won the battle.

She felt herself slipping further and further out of control. Duncan's strokes grew bolder, enflaming her senses. His whispered words soothed her heart. His intoxicating scent mixed with hers drenched them in the fragrance of forbidden desire. She drew him to her lips, and the taste of their kiss only drew out the hunger their bodies craved. When she opened her eyes, his intense stare staked his claim. His statement resonated in her heart.

Selina trembled as her body grew tighter. She pressed herself into his hand, her body begging for the unknown. Only Duncan knew how to ease the ache consuming her.

"Duncan," she moaned.

"Yes, my love?" he teased and bit at her neck.

"Please," she groaned.

"Please what, my love?" His mouth trailed above the neckline of her dress. His tongue dipping in between the swell of her breasts.

Selina didn't know what she pleaded. While his touch pleasured her, Selina held onto her sanity by a thin thread. His lips tortured her body with exquisite caresses, and she forgot everything. Because nothing else mattered in this moment but them. She could rationalize her actions later. For now, she only wanted Duncan to satisfy her body's demands.

"Please this?" Duncan asked, sliding in another finger. He guided them in and out in a slow motion, each glide slower than the last.

"Or perhaps please this?" His fingers quickened and slid in farther, each glide faster and deeper than the last.

Each stroke was relentless in drawing out her pleasure. Selina's body shook in his hold, drawing closer to her release. His mouth closed over hers before she screamed her pleasure. His kiss was as demanding as the strokes of his fingers. She came undone on his lap, her gratification rocking him to his core. Her eyelids fluttered open, and the look in them shocked him. He didn't believe it was possible, but even Selina couldn't deny what her gaze held. Its unspoken declaration would set the precedence on how Duncan proceeded on his quest to win Selina's love.

Just the thought of another man, let alone his cousin, drawing forth Selina's desires set him on the edge of an uncontrollable emotion where there were no words to describe its force. It only fueled his need to lead them down a destructible path of temptation where neither of them denied their desires.

"And he never will," Duncan growled.

In the aftermath of her pleasure, Duncan's comment confused Selina. "Who?"

Duncan brushed the stray curls that had come undone behind her ear. "Lucas."

Selina stiffened in Duncan's embrace. What had she done? Her eyes widened as they traveled the length of her body. Her dress rose to her knees where Duncan's hands had been moments before, caressing her into a frenzy. She shifted on his lap, lowering her gown in shock, and the back of her legs pressed into his hardness. She gasped and tried to push herself out of his arms. Duncan's grip tightened, but in her determination to get away, her knee connected with his most sensitive parts. With a groan, he reluctantly released her. She scrambled to her feet, stepping back until she hit the fountain.

She pressed her hands against her cheeks. The full brunt of what she'd allowed him to do settled over her. Her head swiveled back and forth, anxiously glancing around to see if anyone caught sight of them. The mortification of her wanton acts should have shamed her, but when her gaze connected with Duncan's, her body only ached to have him consume her. Heart and soul.

Duncan prowled toward Selina, drawing her hands from her face and holding them in his. He understood her fear of someone noticing them and wanted to ease her worries. He'd risked their standings in his family with his blatant disregard of decorum. However, he didn't regret one second, nor would he regret pursuing her. They were meant for each other alone.

"Unhand me." Selina tried tugging her hands away.

"Never."

Selina growled. "It can never be. Now step away before someone comes upon us."

Duncan stared her down, refusing her demand. When her gaze kept flittering around to see if they were alone, he took pity on her. But not before stating his intention on where they stood. "You are mine, and no other man will treat you to the pleasures I gave you. Certainly not Lucas. He does not deserve you, but I do. And I will not stop until you are mine." He stepped back for her to make an escape.

But Selina never moved a step. Instead, she stood her ground, narrowing her gaze. The audacity of him to assume she was his toy to declare ownership of. He might have shown her an insight into how their passion enflamed when stroked, but she was her own woman. Not his or any other man's. She was tired of controlling men and their demands. The more she thought of how everyone tried to control her, the more her fury grew.

Duncan stood before her, wearing a smug smile of satisfaction. Over the past few months, she had allowed him to place doubt in her mind on the destiny of her life. Well, no more. Before Selina even realized her intention, she let her fury get the best of her and slapped Duncan across the face. The resounding hit echoed around the garden, silencing the peacefulness of nature with its declaration.

Duncan raised his hand up to caress where she had acted with violence, but his smile only grew more confident. "What I stated is not a threat, but a promise, my love."

"I am not your love," Selina hissed before stalking away.

Oh, but you are. Duncan chuckled, watching Selina storm back toward the house. He wished to follow her, but it would only rile her more and draw attention their way. Attention he wasn't ready for yet, not until she made her own declaration of love to him. Then he would declare his intentions, but not until then.

"Oh, Duncan, what are you doing?"

Duncan stilled at the question. He closed his eyes and winced. Abigail was the last person he wanted to witness him with Selina. He didn't wish to get her hopes up, in case he couldn't succeed with his plans.

He opened his eyes and swung around, trying to charm her with a smile. "Whatever do you mean?"

She shook her head at him. "Leave your innocent act for someone who does not know you any better."

"I only wonder what you might have witnessed."

"Enough."

Duncan quirked a brow. "Enough of what?"

"Enough to draw a dreaded conclusion of a catastrophe hanging in the balance of crumbling."

Duncan took a step back, clutching his chest. "It sounds morbid."

Abigail paused. "Actually, now that I ponder what I saw, it appears most spectacular."

Duncan winced again when Abagail declared her opinion. "Perhaps you misinterpreted what you saw."

Abigail shook her head. "No, I do not believe I did."

Duncan stumbled to explain what she might have seen. Before he could gloss over his time with Selina, Abigail continued on, not allowing him time to deceive her. "I didn't believe Gemma when she told me how Selina was not a threat. That her feelings lie with another. You are the other gentleman Selina holds feelings for. I saw it with my own eyes."

Duncan humphed. "Did you not witness her slap and the fury of her words? Not to mention how she stalked away. I believe, dear cousin, the air from London has affected the way you are processing your thoughts. It is a good thing you have returned to the fresh country air."

Abigail chuckled and rested her hands on the back of the bench he'd held Selina on. Obviously, Abigail hadn't witnessed that exchange. "I am not your cousin, Duncan Forrester. However, I am your friend, and if I could offer you a bit of advice?"

"And that would be?"

"Proceed with caution."

Duncan laughed. "Oh, I can handle a broken heart."

Abigail walked by Duncan before replying. "But I do not think she can."

Abigail walked away before Duncan could question her further about what she had witnessed. Her cryptic warning confused him. Had she witnessed Selina's reaction to him? Also, she left before he could warn her not to wish for a different outcome where Lucas was concerned. The only fact he held confidence in was how Selina would never suffer from a broken heart. Because he had no intention of breaking her heart.

~~~~~~

From the window, Susanna watched Selina stalk out of the garden. "Oh, she looks quite upset. Do you suppose she had a confrontation with one of the girls?"

Theo sighed. "She does at that. I hope not. But the girls have shown no sign of welcoming her, as I hoped they would have. I thought when Gemma befriended Selina, the rest would follow, but unfortunately, they have not."

"I am afraid they are finding it difficult to put the past behind them. And with the wedding drawing closer, it is only making them tenser."

Theo pinched his lips, drumming his fingers on the woodwork around the window. "I thought I convinced the two married ones to help our case."

"Perhaps ye recruited the wrong individuals to aid in your mad caper," drawled a voice from behind them.

Susanna gasped, spinning around. Her face lit up with joy at the handsome gentleman standing in the doorway. She ran across the room and into his welcoming arms like a young debutante smitten with a beau. He wrapped her in his arms and swung her around, kissing her like a starving man.

Theo gave a discreet cough. "You are not setting a proper example for my wards by this display of affection."

The gentleman lifted his head and pierced Colebourne with a stare. "As if I give a shite. I've heard plenty of your wards' indiscretions this season. My kiss was tame compared to theirs."

Colebourne laughed. "So true, Forrester."

Susanna pressed her hand against her husband's cheek. "You came."

"Aye, lass. I figured if you two planned to arrange my son's life, I had best meet the lass you plan to chain him to."

Susanna tugged on his hand and led him to the settee. "You will love her, Ramsay. She is the perfect woman for Duncan. She will always keep him on his toes."

Forrester smirked. "I met the lass. Lucas should be so lucky to gain her as a bride. But your family's loss shall be our gain."

Colebourne quirked an eyebrow. "So what is your opinion of Lady Selina?"

Forrester sighed. "She appears as a lady who wears the weight of the world on her shoulders. She is not what I expected from our correspondence, my love." He lifted Susanna's hand to his lips.

Susanna blushed. "I fear I did not do Selina justice. It was not until days before the engagement dinner when I realized her true character. This family has shown her a great injustice with their misunderstanding. I hold myself responsible for not seeing her vulnerability sooner."

Colebourne lowered himself onto a chair opposite of them. "We are both at fault, Susanna. I have known the girl her entire life and did not see how lonely and miserable she was. Norbury is a sad excuse for a father. And he will be our greatest obstacle in this match."

Forrester scoffed. "Norbury has always been a fool."

"But smart enough to trap me into an agreement that has made Lucas and Selina both miserable. I must put a stop to it."

"So my son is to be your sacrifice," Forrester growled.

Susanna tried to calm her husband. "No, dear. Selina has enamored Duncan with her lovely charm. You must see the sparks that fly between them."

"Humph."

Colebourne pinched his lips. "If you will not take our word for it, then you shall see for yourself at dinner."

"Not this evening. I am sore from the carriage ride, and I only want a hot bath and some warm food. Perhaps tomorrow." Forrester stood, pulling Susanna up with him.

"I take it I am to lose my chaperone for the evening too?" called Colebourne, stopping them before they left.

"Aye. You steal my wife away for months on end. Ye can deal with your entire brood for one evening by yourself."

Colebourne laughed. "If I must."

Forrester chuckled. "You must. And do not tell a soul I have arrived. I want to surprise the boy myself tomorrow."

Colebourne nodded and smiled as he watched them leave. Ah, he missed his late wife, Olivia. But he found joy that his sister-in-law still enjoyed a loving marriage with Forrester. Now he only needed to settle Susanna and Ramsay's son into a loving marriage of his own.

Chapter Eight

Selina slipped out of the servant's entrance, carrying a small basket and her breakfast wrapped up in a piece of linen. She rested the basket along with a book on a bench outside of the garden. The fresh morning air and the music of the birds beckoned her to enjoy her breakfast in the splendid glory of the garden. Without realizing where her steps took her, Selina wandered toward the bench where Duncan had held her in his arms and given her a decadent taste of the passion flowing between them.

She settled on the bench and nibbled away on the pastries the cook had prepared for her. She wanted to avoid another disappointing morning where the other ladies didn't extend an invitation for her to join their breakfast ritual. Also, she wished to evade her father and his morning lectures on how to instigate herself into Colebourne's household. Selina couldn't endure breakfast with Lucas ignoring her, the pity glances of Colebourne and Lady Forrester, and the piercing gaze of Duncan. Already one week into her stay, and her upcoming position in the family had been no more accepted than before.

A rabbit scurried out from behind the bushes and paused nearby. He nibbled on a blade of grass, oblivious to Selina's dilemma.

Selina sighed. "What am I to do?"

Her spoken whisper startled the rabbit. It bounced away, on to a quieter destination. Oh, how Selina wished she could do the same.

Unfortunately, her destiny awaited her, no matter how hard she tried to resist it. Which left her wondering if she could surrender to the passion Duncan tempted her with and discover where it might lead them. Once she declared her vows to Gray, she wouldn't dishonor them. Since Gray and Selina were bound to a promise now, was it still dishonorable? It didn't stop Gray from holding affections for another, nor would it stop him after they wed. Gray would continue to love Abigail Cason. So why shouldn't Selina create special memories to treasure in the years to come? Perhaps then she could endure the loneliness her marriage to Gray would eventually succumb to.

A throat cleared. "I see I am not the only one Cook sneaks her best pastries to."

Selina smiled at the friendly gentleman from the day before. "Shh. Another secret of mine I must ask for you to keep."

He winked. "I shall guard your secrets for a peek at what Cook gifted you with this morning."

Selina patted the spot next to her. "Only if you promise to share if your fare is tastier than mine."

He chuckled. "Ah, a lass who knows how to negotiate. Whatever gentleman wins your heart will always have to be one step ahead of you."

Selina's smile disappeared. She knew he meant no harm in his comment. However, it only drove home the point of her demise. She swiftly regained her smile at his frown of distress. Her own distress wasn't to make him feel uncomfortable.

She opened her linen to display the few pastries she had remaining. "I am afraid I have little to offer you. They were much too delicious to stop from passing between my lips."

He sat down, opening his own linen. "I must confess I ate a few of mine on my trek from the kitchen."

"Oh, Cook must favor you more. She gave you her treasured apple-filling pastries."

"Ahh, lass, I disagree. She favored you with her cream-filled ones coated with sugar. You are obviously her favorite."

Selina giggled. "Perhaps since we like the other's treats, I can persuade you to switch linens."

"Ah, my lady, I need no persuasion if you are offering those delicious apple treats."

She passed over her linen to him. "Please, call me Selina."

"Then you must call me Ramsay." He offered his linen to Selina.

"With pleasure." She bit into a pastry, and her eyes closed as she enjoyed the savory treat. "Mmm, most divine."

"I could not agree with you more. So what draws you outside this fine morning? I bet the spread inside is much grander."

"But not the company," Selina muttered.

Ramsay laughed hard. "No, I do not suppose so."

Selina blushed a bright red. "Oh, please forgive my bluntness. It was most unladylike of me."

"'Tis no need to apologize, lass. I am well aware of the company and fully understand your need for a peaceful morning."

"'Tis not as if they are …"

"Selina, lass. Like I said, no explanation is necessary. So were the pastries worth the trade?"

Selina licked the sugar off her fingers. "Very much so."

Ramsay nodded, relaxing back against the bench. "Excellent."

They shared their breakfast, enjoying the silence of the morning. Before long, Ramsay started sharing stories of his life in Scotland. It sounded like a glorious place to live. One without the stricture of society and its rules to act the proper lady. Selina longed to venture to such an uninhibited place where no one cared who she was or who she married.

Selina sighed. "It sounds like heaven."

Ramsay humphed. "Aye, but also a dangerous country to wander if one does not hold a clue to where one is traveling."

"Still, I hope to visit Scotland one day."

"Perhaps you will."

Selina narrowed her gaze. "So you recommend that I hire a guide if I wish to run away to Scotland?"

"If you decide to run away, I have just the lad in mind to help lead the way."

Selina frowned. "You would not guide me to your paradise?"

"Nay. 'Fraid the wife would not take too kindly to me running away with another lass. Even one as friendly as you, my dear."

Selina slapped her cheeks. "Oh, I … At least … I did not mean ..."

Ramsay patted her arm. "I know ye did not mean for me to steal away with ye. I am only teasin' ye, lass. But ye say the word and I will help ye sneak away."

Selina's lips trembled. "If it were only that simple."

"I take it you have not made your decision."

"No. Every time I convince myself to grab a piece of happiness, my conscience speaks its demands."

"Sometimes the conscience is only the voice of others who have engrained their beliefs into how you perceive your thoughts. Therefore, your actions lead you to benefit them. If you were to ignore your conscience, would you make a grab for your happiness?"

"Yes," Selina whispered.

"Then my advice to ye is to grab your happiness, even if it is only for a short spell. Do not pass up the opportunity to follow your heart. Because ye may not get the chance again."

"Did you?"

Ramsay smiled widely. "Yes, and I never looked backed once."

Selina was about to question Ramsay when she heard Duncan calling out her name. Her eyes widened with panic. Even though she was almost ready to give into her desires with him, she wasn't ready to face him. Especially this early in the morning, when she didn't have her wits about her. Whenever she wasn't herself, he invaded her senses, and she was powerless to resist him.

Selina quickly came to her feet. "I fear I must leave. Thank you for breaking fast with me, Ramsay. I hope we can do this again during your stay."

Before Selina heard Ramsay's response, she took off in the opposite direction from where Duncan called her name. "Oh, we will break many breakfasts together, lass, in our time to come."

"Selina," Duncan shouted as he came into the clearing. "You!"

Ramsay nodded. "Me."

Duncan growled. "What are you doing here?" He glanced around, hoping to spot Selina. In his distraction, he missed the devious grin on his father's face.

Ramsay stood up. "Is that how ye welcome your father?"

Duncan wrapped his father in a hug. "Sorry, Athair. Welcome. Your presence took me by surprise. I was not aware of your arrival."

"I asked your mother to keep her silence until I settled in."

Duncan walked around, glancing down the different paths. "Did you come for the wedding?"

"Looking for someone, my boy?"

Duncan shook his head. "No. I only thought I overheard you conversing with another."

"Really? I thought you were calling for a lass named Selina."

Duncan raised a brow. "Your point, Father?"

Ramsay laughed. "No point, son. Only wondering why you search for your cousin's fiancée."

"Because mother asked for me to find her since Selina never made an appearance at breakfast."

Ramsay narrowed his gaze. "Your mother, aye? You would not be trifling with the lass's affections, would ye? Did ye not learn anything from the very thing ye had to run away from? If it were not for your uncle's generosity, ye would find yourself married to another lass at this moment."

Duncan ran his hand through his hair in frustration. "You do not understand, old man."

"Then help me make sense of why ye are pursuing Selina Pemberton."

Duncan slumped onto the bench. "If mother had found herself intended to wed another man, would ye have stopped your pursuit to make her yours?"

"Ahh, so that be the reason."

Duncan swiped a hand down his face. "Aye."

Ramsay laughed, sitting back down. "I can understand your smitten infatuation."

Duncan frowned, looking at the linens. "She was here."

Ramsay nodded. "Aye. But she fled when ye called out her name. I wonder why that would be."

"I only have two weeks to show her how rare a love like ours is."

"Has she expressed her love to you?"

"No. She does not realize it yet."

Ramsay shook his head. "So you plan to force it with your impatience?"

"I am running out of time."

"Perhaps if you pull back from your prowess and show her the kindness she is not receiving from this family, you just might burrow your way into her heart."

"They do not understand her the way I do. They are too clouded from her actions in the past to see her vulnerability."

Ramsay gripped Duncan's shoulder. "I know, son. With your love, they will soon see the treasure she is."

Duncan peered into his father's gaze. "You see it, do you not?"

"Aye. And your mother and I could not approve more."

Duncan nodded. "Do ye know where she ran off to?"

Ramsay laughed. "Nay. You are on your own to discover where she fled to. But Cook told me how she prepared a basket of her chocolate biscuits for your young lass. And I saw the basket and a book resting on a bench near the garden's entrance. Perhaps you can bribe Cook with some candy from the village to have her tell you what Selina's plans are."

Duncan jumped off the bench and strode off toward the path.

"Duncan?"

He paused, turning back to his father. "Aye?"

"Good luck, my boy. I have a feeling you will need a lot of it."

"Ahh, but you are forgetting. Luck is my middle name. After all, I am a Forrester, and we make our own luck." With a cocky grin, he sauntered away to catch his lass.

"Aye, we do at that, my boy," Ramsay murmured, watching his son chase after the lass of his dreams. "That we do."

Chapter Nine

Duncan strode along the path at a brisk pace. He wanted to take his horse to reach Selina quicker after he'd learned from Cook where Selina had ventured to, but he didn't want to draw attention to himself. If he ran into Lucas, then his cousin would demand to ride along with him. He found his time spent with Lucas became more difficult, the stronger his feelings toward Selina grew. He was committing the ultimate betrayal by pursuing his cousin's intended. However, Lucas held no regard for Selina. In fact, Lucas's cool treatment toward Selina fueled Duncan's pursuit. Lucas's affections lay with Abigail, but Selina didn't deserve his indifference. And the more he watched Selina withdraw into herself by his family's treatment, the more he wanted to steal her away to Scotland.

His steps slowed once he came into the opening. He stopped in his tracks when he saw Selina holding hands and skipping in a circle with a group of young girls. The smile lighting her face and the carefree joy she exhibited warmed his heart. This was the true Selina she kept hidden from everyone. He wondered *why*. Why hold herself back from her true character?

Duncan leaned against the tree and watched her. He was far enough away where she couldn't spot him. He was glad he had walked. The children would have seen his horse, interrupting Selina's time with them.

They twirled around faster and faster in their circle and soon fell to the ground. Their giggles reached him, and he released a burst of laughter. Selina lay on her back, pointed at the clouds, and started talking. Soon each girl pointed at the sky for Selina to look above. She smiled at them, and her lips formed a small circle of surprise, which brightened the child's face. After a while, they sat up and started picking the surrounding wildflowers. Duncan slid down and sat back against the tree once he realized Selina meant to spend her morning playing with the girls.

Selina sat among them as if she were their friend. They talked, giggled, and sat in silence while they played with the flowers. He wished he could listen to them. Perhaps learn the depth of the lady who entranced him under her spell with her every act.

The smallest lass of the group jumped up, ran behind Selina, and laid a crown of flowers upon Selina's head. Selina smiled at the young tyke and reached to hug her from behind.

"I declare you the master crown builder for the day," Selina announced.

The other girls erupted into laughter while the girl gave Selina a shy smile. Then Selina whispered into the girl's ear, and she ran off to do Selina's bidding. Once the young girl left, Selina proclaimed her pride at the other girls' designs.

The girl came back, lugging a basket behind her. Selina rose to help her when she saw her struggles. She sat back down with the basket on her lap and opened the lid. Duncan knew the cook had packed chocolate biscuits for Selina. She closed the lid and asked the girls a question. He listened to their moans of disgust. Then Selina opened the lid again and took another peek. She asked another question, and they answered with delight, jumping up from the ground. Selina laughed with pure abandonment. Duncan ached for her to enjoy herself with him in the same manner.

Selina drew out a tin and passed it around the group. Once it returned to her, she counted out the remaining biscuits and passed the tin around again. A wave of arms rose to draw a chocolate biscuit into each girl's mouth. His mouth watered to taste one of the delicious treats. After they finished eating their snacks, Selina rose with the basket. Each of the girls followed her lead. She held out her hand to the girl who'd gifted her with the flowered crown, and they walked toward the cottages. Duncan wandered closer when Selina rounded the corner.

A group of ladies sat around a small table drinking tea. It wasn't the elaborate setup his peers would enjoy, but one of ladies who worked hard to keep a home for their families. He was more than friendly with the families who lived on his uncle's land. Duncan and Lucas spent a lot of time helping these families build their cottages and assisting them when they fell into hard times. He wasn't aware Selina knew them so intimately, and he bet Lucas didn't know either. But he would raise his bet that his uncle knew of Selina's activities. It was the reason Uncle Theo encouraged them to give her a chance because there were hidden sides to Selina's character she never showed them.

Selina hung back while the young girls exclaimed their enjoyment at Selina's visit. Each mother smiled with pleasure and paid Selina their gratitude for keeping the girls entertained. Soon Selina found herself ushered into a chair and engaged with the ladies while the girls ran inside their homes. Soon they descended upon them again with dolls in their hands and gathered in a group to play.

Duncan rubbed his heart as he watched them accept Selina for who she was, not for what others expected her to be. He never realized how one could love someone so profoundly where they ached for the other's sorrow. Now he understood the heartache Selina suffered, and he wanted to ease it any way possible. His plan to steal her away became more real—and more foolish. Because no matter how far they ran, she would still suffer.

One of the little girls rose and started skipping toward her mother when she tripped and fell. She started crying for her mama, but her mother's hands were full rocking a baby.

Selina stood and held out her arms. "Let me hold the babe. I have not had the chance to welcome your newborn."

The mother handed the baby off to Selina. "You are so dear."

Selina sat in the chair and rocked the baby back and forth, cooing into the blanket. A serene smile lit her face. Her fingers caressed its soft hair, and the baby's hand tightened around Selina's finger. Before long, she started humming a lullaby to the baby, soothing its whimpers. Once the baby grew quiet, she whispered a story to the other children. The young girl who fell had fallen asleep in her mother's arms. The mother rose, and Duncan stepped forward, taking the lass. He followed the mother inside and laid the girl upon the bed.

Before he left, Mrs. Groves stopped him. "She is a sweet lady who deserves the world."

Duncan nodded. "Aye, that she does."

"Do not hurt her," Mrs. Groves warned.

"I do not plan to."

She shook her head at his refusal. "I see the infatuation in your eyes when you regard her, Lord Forrester. It is only one that will end in heartache for Selina and trouble for your family if you act upon it."

Duncan gulped. "Is it obvious?"

Mrs. Groves sighed. "Yes. Has no one else called you out upon it?"

"Only Charlie and perhaps Gemma. Everyone else is too wrapped up in their own drama to notice."

"And Lord Gray?"

Duncan shook his head. He wouldn't betray Lucas on where his heart lay. That was Lucas's own burden to carry, not Duncan's.

They walked to the door and watched Selina lure the other children into naps with her stories. The other women were clearing away their morning tea.

"She never shows this side of herself to others," whispered Duncan.

"Perhaps she is afraid of how harshly they will judge her."

Duncan turned his head, a questioning frown upon his face. "Why would anyone judge her for showing kindness?"

Mrs. Groves sighed again at having to explain to Duncan what was so plainly obvious. "Perhaps they have already formed an undesirable opinion of her and refuse to look past it to discover what special qualities she is capable of."

"How long has she made these visits?"

Mrs. Groves smiled. "A long time now."

Curiosity lit Duncan's gaze. "Since when?"

Mrs. Groves nodded to the other ladies. "Since we were young girls."

Her answer stunned Duncan. "How?"

Mrs. Groves patted his arm. "'Tis not my story to tell," she answered before helping to clean away the morning tea.

Duncan shook his shock away and followed Mrs. Groves to help carry the other children inside to continue their naps. The older girls helped their mothers gather the leftovers of their mid-morning snack and teacups.

After he carried the last child in, he kept his distance from Selina. He couldn't tear his gaze away from her peaceful nature. She smiled shyly at him before returning her attention to the babe. She didn't see the smile he graced her with, which was for the best. Because then she would have realized the depth of his love for her and run for salvation. It was an emotion she wouldn't understand while she tried to survive where no one wanted her. He promised to make it possible for her to flourish there. He must convince her of his love.

When Duncan stepped out of the shadows to draw Joy from Anna's arms and carry her into the cottage, Selina's heart raced. She should have known when she ran from him this morning that he wouldn't stop his pursuit. She'd sensed someone watching while she played with the girls in the open clearing, but every time she'd searched, she saw no one nearby.

Now he stood near, increasing the pounding of her heart. She wondered what he'd discussed with Anna. They'd stood inside the doorway, and Selina noticed the defense in her Anna's gaze as if she'd warned Duncan away from Selina, a warning the gentleman wouldn't take lightly, for she had tried many times herself. However, once he came closer, he kept a respectable distance away and didn't taunt her as he usually did. Duncan wasn't one to hold his thoughts in front of others. No, he always voiced them no matter who was present. The other ladies wouldn't have mattered to him in the slightest. His new behavior was at odds with his normal character, which only set Selina more on edge around him, leaving her wondering how to handle Duncan.

After Anna finished helping the other ladies, she rushed over to Selina to gather the babe. Selina rose and handed over the precious bundle. She felt joy at Anna's good fortune in delivering another healthy baby girl.

After Anna received the baby from Selina, she thrust the bundle into Duncan's arms, much to his surprise. She drew Selina away and into a hug. Selina returned the gesture, her need for friendly affection strong.

Anna curved her hands around Selina's cheeks and whispered, "Your true destiny is what your heart yearns for. Once you open your heart to your yearnings, only then will you accept your destiny. Do not fight it, only embrace it with open arms."

Selina nodded in understanding, too choked to speak. Anna was the closest she had to a friend. "Your caring advice warms my heart."

"My advice is from one friend to another. What I offer you is the same I would offer any friend of mine."

Selina gasped in shock. She hadn't realized Anna regarded her in that manner.

Anna shook her head in disappointment. "Yes, Selina. We are friends. Our visits over the years are proof of our bond."

"I thought of you as one, but never imagined you considered me the same. No one else ever has," Selina whispered.

Anna brought Selina in for another hug. "Then they are fools."

A tear slid from Selina's eye, and she quickly brushed it away. "I am becoming aware of that myself."

Anna turned toward Duncan, who wiggled the baby around in his arms, trying to calm it from crying. Selina and Anna broke out in giggles at the horrified expression on his face. Anna tsked and gathered the babe in her arms.

"Thank you for your kind help, Lord Forrester. However, I am afraid your services as a nanny is beyond your reach at the moment. But in time, I think you can manage one of your own." Anna winked at Duncan, tilting her head toward Selina.

Her reaction confused Duncan. Because only a short while ago, she'd warned him away from Selina. "As soon as I can convince a certain lass to give me a chance, I will master handling a babe in no time."

"So you say, my lord." She turned to Selina. "We enjoyed your visit. Will we see you next week?"

Selina smiled. "Yes. Also, I have left a tin of chocolate biscuits for the boys once they return from the fields."

Anna laughed. "They will devour them with glee."

Anna walked into her house, leaving Selina alone with Duncan. She gathered up her basket and the book she'd brought with her. Before she strolled too far away, Duncan whisked the items out of her hands to carry.

"May I escort you back to Colebourne Manor?"

"I am not ready to make my return there now." Selina tried to grab back the items he took.

Duncan didn't answer her, but held out his arm, indicating for her to continue walking. Selina refused to fight with him while others could watch. She didn't wish to show them her shrewish behavior that others witnessed. She took off, walking back toward the open clearing, and took a path toward the local village. Selina looked over her shoulder to see if Duncan was following her. The lush grass soaked up the sound of his footsteps. Selina took a detour, leading them near a brook of water.

At first, Duncan thought Selina was leading them toward the village. But their path redirected to a secluded spot. His curiosity for the lass grew once again. How did Selina know this spot even existed? He didn't know her to explore his uncle's lands. But she must, for she knew exactly where to lead them.

Selina lowered the basket next to a rock before she sat upon it. She leaned over and untied the laces on her boots before slipping them off. He gulped when she slid the silk tights off her feet. Selina wiggled her toes in the sun, shooting him a silly smile. She jumped off the rock and dipped her toes into the bubbling brook. Once she realized the warmth of the water, she submerged her entire foot, lifted her skirts, and ventured out farther.

"Who are you?" Duncan whispered.

Chapter Ten

Duncan didn't realize he'd spoken his thoughts until Selina smiled coyly at him.

Selina bent her head and looked at Duncan between her lashes. "Selina Pemberton, my lord." She attempted a curtsy, but lost her balance.

Duncan ripped off his jacket and attempted to peel his boots off, but he slipped on the wet bank. He landed on his rear, and the peal of Selina's laughter echoed around them. She had righted herself, only getting the bottom of her dress wet, and came to his rescue. She looked down at him with delight shining from her eyes. He attempted a growl, which only brought more amusement to her face.

"Oh, dear, Lord Forrester, it appears as if you wrestled the mud and it won." Selina brought her hand up to cover her smile.

Duncan looked down and noticed his once crisp white shirt was now covered in mud and grass stains. It would appear he needed to gather more sweets for the servant who had the task of cleaning his clothes. Since he hadn't brought a valet with him, some poor maid must scrub out the stains. Oh, well, it was worth it to relish her enjoyment.

He gave Selina a sheepish smile before tugging on her ankle. "It would appear so."

She gasped and landed on top of him. One minute Selina teased Duncan, the next she found herself spread across him with his arm circling around her waist. He brought his hand up and swiped her nose with his thumb. She crinkled her nose, peering cross-eyed to see he had smeared a dab of mud on her face.

Duncan gasped for dramatic effect. "Why, Lady Selina, it would appear you have suffered from the same mishap as myself."

Selina's eyes twinkled with revenge, but she never moved a single inch. "No, 'tis only from your brutal treatment that it appears so. Not from my clumsy attempt to save a damsel in distress. One I had to save myself from because a certain lord possessed no skill to act quickly enough. If I am not mistaken, this feels like one of those déjà vu moments."

Duncan shook his head in denial. "Oh, no, you shall not blame me for that incident. That one was truly your fault, which resulted in both of us getting drenched."

Selina pushed herself off Duncan, shaking out her skirts. Water sprayed him in the face, but he didn't care, for he caught a magnificent glance of very shapely legs. Long, slender legs rising to the most tempting sight of pale ivory thighs. Before he took more of her in, she stepped over him and sat down. Selina opened the basket and drew out an apple. Then she picked up her book and started reading while eating, ignoring him as if he were not even there. Duncan chuckled to himself. So that was how it would be?

Duncan pushed himself to his feet. He untied his cravat and tugged his shirt out of his trousers, pulling the muddy garment from his body. He whipped it off, walked to the brook, and dipped it into the water. The clear blue water turned a murky brown. He hunched down and rubbed the shirt together, working out the mud. His gaze wandered back over to find Selina engrossed in her book, flipping a page after reading it and eating the apple. Totally oblivious to him. When it appeared as clean as he could get it, he laid it out across the rock for the warm sun to dry it out, then stretched out on the grass and closed his eyes. He listened to the occasional crunch of an apple and a page turning.

Duncan squinted, turning his head to stare at Selina. She sat cross-legged with the book on her lap and her head bent. She had taken off her bonnet. Her hair had come unbound, and the light breeze lifted the tendrils sweeping across her face. Selina swept them away and tucked them behind her ears, never once taking her eyes off her story. Once again, he wondered who this creature was. It was then he knew the depth of his troubles and how hard he had fallen for Selina. If he imagined he'd fallen in love with her long before, then their stolen time only reaffirmed his feelings, making him fall deeper in love.

This creature differed from the one he'd encountered before. She'd mentioned a moment they shared in the past, where he'd rocked a boat and drowned both of them. He still heard her shrieks of displeasure. However, in his defense, he'd only tried to save her from a bee. And what had he received in return? A set-down that would burn most gentlemen's ears. But not him. No, he found amusement in her tirade. She'd been a most glorious sight that afternoon. Her gown had been soaked and visible to his roving gaze. With each slanderous word she uttered, her bosom heaved in fury. Selina only heightened his desire to have her for himself.

He sighed, turning his head back up to the sky. He would have to shelve his plans to relentlessly pursue and tear down her defenses. His father's advice to treat Selina with kindness and Anna Groves' warning to not break her heart echoed loud and clear. No matter how much he ached to possess her mind, body, and soul, he ached more to learn this side of her character and to become her friend. Duncan tensed, closing his hands into fists at his side, fighting his inner desires. Then he relaxed, accepting the new course he would take to win Selina's heart. He smiled at the new peace he found, and he closed his eyes to enjoy the warmth of a late summer day.

Selina fought to concentrate on reading the book of poems. She hadn't read a single word since she'd opened the book. How could she concentrate when Duncan stripped off his clothing? Well, not all of his clothing, unfortunately. *Unfortunately?* Selina pressed her hand against her cheek and felt the warmth of her wanton thoughts. When Duncan turned, she quickly dropped her hand and turned a page, pretending interest in the book. It took all of her control to eat the apple and pretend he wasn't there. Her mind raced with indecent thoughts of him stripping bare and swimming in the water. Could she show her own bravery by joining him if he acted on her indecent thoughts?

Duncan had caught her unaware when he questioned her on who she was. She wanted to share her true self with him. Not the viper everyone in his family and the ton believed her to be. This was a secret spot she used to escape from the hostility of the Colebourne household. It was the spot where her life had taken an unexpected change, the place where she'd discovered a different life existed from the station her father raised her in. She'd met her first friend here.

Selina peeked out between her lashes to see Duncan relaxing in the sun. A sigh escaped her lips before she could stop it. The only reaction from Duncan was a smile spreading across his face. But not one comment escaped his lips, nor did he turn his head. His eyes remained closed and his body relaxed in the day's warmth.

Oh, but he was most divine. She couldn't stop her gaze from devouring him as her eyes traveled the length of his body, no matter how hard she tried. His broad chest glistened in the sunlight and his bronze skin beckoned her to come near and caress its hard ridges. Duncan wasn't one of your debonair aristocrats who lazed around in the clubs or indulged in hedonistic pleasures. He spent most of his time outdoors, doing physical activities.

Duncan's smile widened when he heard her sigh. "Are you going to share what is inside your basket or am I to starve while watching you consume its contents?"

Selina dug into the basket. "Catch." She threw an apple at him.

Duncan caught the apple and took a bite out of the succulent fruit. "What are you reading?"

"A collection of poetry."

He rolled on his side, propping himself up on one arm. "Read me one."

Selina thumbed through the book to find a poem to read to Duncan. "This is Love's Philosophy by Percy Bysshe Shelley." She cleared her throat and launched into the poem.

"The fountains mingle with the river
  And the rivers with the ocean,
The winds of heaven mix for ever
  With a sweet emotion;
Nothing in the world is single;
  All things by a law divine
In one spirit meet and mingle.
  Why not I with thine?—

"See the mountains kiss high heaven
  And the waves clasp one another;

No sister-flower would be forgiven
  If it disdained its brother;
And the sunlight clasps the earth
  And the moonbeams kiss the sea:
What is all this sweet work worth
  If thou kiss not me?"

Duncan listened to the lyrical sadness in Selina's voice when she read the poem. The words whispered in the wind, drawing forth more questions. Was the poem meant for him to kiss her again? Or did she long for Lucas to kiss her with reassurances of the vows they were to speak soon?

When she raised her gaze to meet his, he saw the longing in them and knew she meant the poem for him alone. Which only made him fight his own longings instead of giving into the pull of her emotions that begged him to fulfill her needs.

When he'd decided to follow the advice of others, it was before Selina had exposed her true self to him. Vulnerabilities and all. But as she showed him more than her vulnerability, she opened herself for him to see her desires. They were for him and no other.

"You have a pleasing voice. Will you read to me some more?"

Selina blushed and nodded. She read more of Shelley and then Wordsworth. Her voice rang clear with the passion written in the poems, as if she had written them. The more she read, the closer he moved toward her, entranced in her spell. Duncan needed to touch her, if only in a friendly gesture. He didn't understand how or why, but he sensed she needed comfort. He needed to be the person to offer it to her, whether as a lover or a friend. Whatever she wanted him to be, he would be that person for her.

Duncan ran his hand down her arm and laced his finger with her hand resting on her knee. His thumb ran along the crease of hers in a gentle stroke. Her words hesitated at his touch, but continued on. On the last verse of the poem, her voice grew shaky. Her eyes drifted to the joining of their hands. He squeezed her fingers, and her gaze rose to meet his. Duncan wished to take away her sorrows into his soul and carry the burden of them.

"Tell me about this spot." He gave her a gentle smile.

"'Tis a long story."

Duncan glanced around. "I have nothing else to occupy my day. Do you?"

Selina giggled. "No, I do not." Then her expression grew pensive. "Nor will anyone miss me."

Duncan wiggled his eyebrows. "Their loss, my gain."

Selina's smile brightened. "When I was around the age of six, I got lost and discovered this spot."

Duncan frowned. "How so?"

"The governess my father hired at the time became infatuated with a local farmer. We would take a walk on the pretense of visiting the village when she actually met with the boy for a secret assignation. They met in a cottage hidden in the trees and ordered me to wait a distance away." Selina pointed through the trees.

"Aye. I know of the cottage. Sinclair's family owns it. They built the cottage for a retired servant who had no other family. Now it sits abandoned and is used whenever Sinclair or any local peers wish for a hunting lodge to escape to."

Selina nodded and raised her brows. "Yes, well, others use the cottage for other activities. One day, I grew bored from waiting, and it was hot standing in the sun. I had seen this brook when we passed through and wanted a drink. So I ventured closer and heard laughter. When I came upon the brook, I saw Anna and some other girls with their mothers. I remember Anna's mother rushed toward me, questioning me on who I was and why I was alone. But I stayed silent, too afraid to tell her. My governess had warned me if I told on her indiscretions, no one would ever like me."

Duncan swore explicitly, causing Selina to blush at his vulgarity. He motioned for her to continue.

"Her threat was not what stopped me, but watching how the young girls played happily with each other and their mothers. They expressed such joy with each other. I had seen nothing like it before. I have no memories of my mother. My father never allowed me to play with other children, except for Lucas. At my young age, I was confused at the dynamics of why he could be my friend when no other child could."

Duncan growled, hanging on to his anger by a thread, but tried to keep it under control so he could listen to Selina's story.

"Soon Anna came over to me and grabbed my hand. She helped me off with my shoes and stockings. When her mother realized her intentions, she helped to tie my dress up, so as not to get wet. Then Anna led me into the water. I remember standing there and feeling a sense of something I had never felt before."

Duncan whispered, "What was that?"

Selina gave him a bittersweet smile. "Happiness."

"Ah, love. That is all I wish to give you." Duncan couldn't help himself. He needed her to know.

Selina lifted her other hand to his cheek. "I know. But 'tis not your responsibility. Soon, that will lie with another."

"Will you allow me the privilege during this fleeting passage of time we have together?" Duncan pleaded.

"Yes." Then Selina surprised him by leaning forward and placing a soft kiss against his lips before pulling back and continuing her story.

"When my governess never showed to find me, Anna's mother took me home with them and sent word to the duke. Colebourne, not wanting to alarm my father of my disappearance, showed up to collect me himself. He saw the change in my demeanor and arranged for me to play with Anna and the other girls during my visits to the estate. However, after a few visits, my father learned of my new friends and forbade me to visit with them again. He kept a tight restriction on my activities whenever we visited Colebourne Manor."

"So how did you come about playing with the young children today?"

Selina shook her head with a teasing grin on her face. "So impatient. You must let me continue." She pulled her hand from his and rummaged in the basket. She pulled out another tin, opened it, and set it on his lap. "Eat. While I weave a tale," Selina demanded.

Duncan pulled out a chunk of cheese, split it into two, and handed Selina a piece. "Is it a tale?"

Selina nibbled a bite before responding. "No. 'Tis but a glimpse into my soul."

Duncan nodded, handing Selina pieces of food to eat in between the telling of her story. He listened, absorbing each scrap of knowledge he could of Selina.

"Well, a few years later, as you know, chaos descended on Colebourne Manor when your cousins lost their parents and moved in. It was an opportunity my father allowed for me to spend in the company of other girls. Like a fool, I thought they would grant me the same acceptance as Anna and her friends. Instead, they excluded me from their tight-knit group. I never understood how they only protected their broken hearts against the grief they suffered from losing their parents. But with each year passing, their rejection kept stinging, so I lashed out at them. Each time more vindictive than the last."

"You mentioned you now understand they only acted out with grief. When did you realize their sufferings affected their actions?"

Selina cringed. "When Lady Langdale came to me and threatened to expose our kiss at the Kanfold Ball, I agreed to take part in her blackmail scheme to ruin Gemma to protect my standing in society. However, when Lady Langdale compared herself to me, shame overwhelmed me. I vowed then to stop her and atone for my past behavior. However, as you have noticed, I have made little progress on that front."

Duncan attempted a smile. "No, but give them time. I am proud of the steps you have taken to make a change. And in time, they will too."

"Yes. Your uncle gave me some similar advice."

"Was today your first visit back to Anna?"

"Ah, lad, ye must learn patience." Selina attempted a Scottish accent, but it fell flat.

Duncan roared with laughter. She kept surprising him today. Who knew Selina Pemberton held a sense of humor? She sat across from him, smirking, and he wanted to absorb her smirk into his soul. He leaned over and captured her lips. He nibbled playfully until she sighed into his kiss and opened her mouth under his. Soon his teasing built into the passion that always grew out of control whenever they kissed.

He pulled her onto his lap, his hands diving into her hair. His mouth ravished her, drawing forth moans, fueling his desires higher. The tongues clashed, devouring each other, wanting to explore where their passion might lead them. When Selina caressed his chest, he thought he might explode. Her exploration set a path of fire from one touch to the next.

Selina pressed into Duncan, her body aching for his hands to explore her as hers did him. His body was crafted with a statue's perfection. Hard and unmovable. But he held her with the gentleness of an angel. His kiss started out playful, but now devoured Selina with a passion she no longer wanted to deny.

She wanted Duncan Forrester any way she could have him.

Before Selina could explore his body anymore, he pulled away from their kiss and grabbed her hands. He brought them to his lips and placed kisses on them. Then he stretched their bodies out and cradled her into his arms. At her frown, he placed a kiss upon it. "Finish your story, lass, while I still have a hold on my resistance."

"What if I no longer wish to deny our attraction?"

Duncan growled. "Selina, I am trying with everything I have in me to respect your boundaries. Do not tempt me. Now finish your story, or I will walk away."

Selina pondered Duncan's words. Why was he fighting their attraction when only yesterday he'd stated his intention to steal her from Lucas? Had he changed his mind? Their kiss spoke otherwise. Even now, he held her like something precious to treasure. Duncan was a walking contradiction she wanted to understand. She didn't wish for him to leave, which only left her to finish her story.

"Very well. Once your cousins settled into their new home, my father was unaware of how they did not welcome me into their inner circle. He thought I filled my days with them. My absence for hours on end went unnoticed by him and everyone else. By then, I had become most skilled on a horse. It was then I learned one of Colebourne's groomsman was Anna's brother. He remembered my visits and helped me to see Anna and her friends again. So I reacquainted with them, and they welcomed me as if I had never disappeared. Never once asking about my absence, only letting me spend time with them. This continued over the years. Since then, they have married and started their families while I watched. I hold out hope that I can share my family with them as they have shared their families with me. Never once did I envy them. I only felt joy when they found love."

Duncan feathered his fingers through Selina's hair. "Anna is very protective of you."

Selina sighed. "All for good reasons. I have cried out my sorrows on her shoulders over the years. It was not until today that I realized she considered me a friend."

Duncan frowned. "Why would she not?"

Selina shrugged. "I didn't understand the meaning of friendship. But now I do. I only hope I can return the gesture as strongly as she does to me."

Duncan's smile was full of reassurance. "I think you already do, lass."

Selina smiled, laying her head against Duncan's chest. His smile grew once he realized Selina had drifted off to sleep in his arms. She clung to him, never loosening her hold. He pulled her closer and thought over the story she told him.

He'd never imagined the true depth of her loneliness until today.

Chapter Eleven

A dark cloud drifted over them, bringing forth a gust of cool wind. As much as Duncan enjoyed holding Selina, they needed to return to Colebourne Manor as soon as possible.

"Love, I am afraid you must awaken." He pressed a kiss to her head.

"Mmm?" She lifted her drowsy lids at him.

He looked up at the sky. "I am afraid we are about to be rained upon if we do not return soon."

Selina gasped when a raindrop landed on her cheek. She jumped up and ran over to her footwear, pulling them on quickly. By the time she finished, Duncan had pulled his shirt on, with his cravat hanging out of the pocket of his suit coat he had flung over his shoulder. He held the basket in his other hand.

"My book?" Selina looked around on the ground.

Duncan held up the basket. "I placed it inside for safekeeping."

Selina nodded, and they took off toward Colebourne Manor. The closer they drew, the more their luck wore thin. So far, only a light drizzle fell, but the sky drew darker, warning them a downpour was inevitable. Duncan slowed his steps for Selina to keep pace with him. The raindrops grew larger, and when Duncan looked behind him, Selina was on his heels with her hair hanging in wet strands. He silently cursed. He must sneak

Selina into the manor with no one catching a glimpse of them. Their appearance would draw too many questions.

They were near the long entrance when Duncan heard a carriage behind them. He drew Selina back toward the trees. He thought he had escaped their notice, but the carriage stopped on the road.

The door swung open, and Charlie shouted over the thunder, "Are you mad for taking a walk in this weather?"

Duncan swung Selina up into his arms and carried her over to the carriage. He leaned in and plunked her down on the empty seat. "We were trying to return before the storm hit."

Duncan climbed into the carriage and sat next to Selina. He looked her way, but she avoided his gaze, trying to put a safe distance between them. He sighed and sat back in his seat. When he met Charlie's gaze, she raised her brows in question before she snickered her delight at catching him and Selina alone. Sinclair shook his head at his wife. Nobody said a word until the carriage drew up before the steps.

Before the servant reached the door, Sinclair nodded toward Duncan's coat and tipped his head toward Selina. "Perhaps you should lend Lady Selina your coat before we go inside."

Duncan looked over to see his muddy handprints on Selina's gown. He closed his eyes and cringed. "I am sorry for damaging your garment."

Selina looked down and blushed at her muddy dress. She pulled his coat around her. "Thank you," she whispered.

Charlie sat forward and buttoned the coat around Selina. Her nemesis took such glee in Selina's demise. She feared the reaction they would receive when they entered the manor. Selina hoped their arrival went unnoticed. The gentleman disembarked from the carriage and helped the ladies to the ground.

Selina's gaze met Duncan's when she tried to pull her hand from his, but he held on. The turbulent emotions—regret, sorrow, but, most of all, passion still denied in his gaze—struck her. When Sinclair cleared his throat, Duncan released her hand and stepped away, no longer meeting her gaze. Selina fell in step next to Charlie as they climbed the stairs and entered the manor, with the gentlemen falling behind them.

Lady Forrester met them with worried excitement. She rushed forward, giving orders to the servants to ready warm baths for Selina and Duncan.

"Oh, you poor dears. Caught in the storm, were you?" Lady Forrester tried to usher Selina toward the stairs.

However, Selina's father's demands kept her still. "Where were you, Selina? And why were you gallivanting around with Forrester when Gray needed your attention?"

"I was … That is …" Selina stuttered out.

"Speak as a lady, not as a village simpleton." Norbury scowled.

"The rain caught…" Selina began.

Charlie interrupted Selina before she delivered an explanation. "I am afraid I am to blame for Selina's disheveled appearance."

Norbury narrowed his gaze. "How so?"

"I invited Selina for a visit this morning."

Norbury pointed at Selina. "That does not explain why she wears Forrester's coat."

Charlie smiled, tilting her head to the side while she continued with her explanation. "Lord Forrester had paid a call on my husband this morning to discuss horseflesh. While we were enjoying tea outdoors, Jasper's mother needed my attention. Before I could return to Selina, the rain fell. Selina rushed to hurry, but slipped on the terrace."

Sinclair slapped Duncan on the back. "Duncan heard Selina's cries and came to her rescue. He ushered her inside and offered his coat for warmth. However, it was not before the rain drenched her. We are only happy Selina suffered no harm from her mishap."

"Oh, what a horrible morning for you, Selina dear. Let me help you to your bedchamber." Lady Forrester wrapped her arm around Selina's waist and guided her away before her father found any flaws in the Sinclairs' fabricated story.

However, before they climbed the stairs, her father halted them. "Selina?"

They turned toward him. "Yes, Father?"

His gaze remained narrow, not quite believing the story he was told. "Until you wed Gray, I think it would be best if you remain close to the manor."

Selina nodded. "Yes, Father."

When the Duke of Norbury issued his demand to Selina, he stalked away, not sparing Duncan a single glance. He breathed a sigh of relief. If Norbury had peered at Duncan, he would have noticed the dire state of his clothing.

Duncan watched his mother guide Selina to her bedchamber. Selina's expression of shock stood out on her features. He tried to keep a calm appearance, but Charlie shocked him too. He thought Charlie would seek her vengeance against Selina, but instead, she'd made excuses for her absence. Duncan stayed silent, trying not to draw attention to himself and his clothing.

Once the foyer cleared, he turned to Charlie and Sinclair. Charlie burst out laughing at his predicament. Sinclair bit back a smile and shrugged at Duncan.

"Oh, you owe me, Duncan Forrester. I cannot wait to collect." Charlie rubbed her hands together in glee.

Duncan gritted his teeth. "I do not understand why you covered for Selina. Nor do I want to know. I only wish to thank both of you for not destroying her."

"I did not do it for you, Forrester, but for Lady Selina. The grievances I held toward the miss are forgotten. Nor does she deserve Norbury's wrath," declared Sinclair.

Duncan raised a brow at Charlie. "And you? Do you promise not to seek your revenge at a later time against Selina?"

Charlie smiled mischievously. "My issues with Selina are in the past."

Duncan didn't quite believe Charlie's easy forgiveness for Selina's past cruelty. This conduct differed from Charlie's usual behavior. He wondered what her game was and how she would attempt to victimize Selina.

"Why do I hold no trust in your actions?"

Charlie shrugged. "Perhaps because you feel guilty for trifling with Selina and want to direct your guilt toward others."

Duncan scowled. "I am not trifling with Selina."

Sinclair placed his hands in between Duncan and Charlie. "Quiet. You can have this discussion later. Anyone could hear this conversation and draw forth more questions. My advice to you, Forrester, is to hurry to your room and change before someone notices your clothing. And you, Lady

Sinclair, I believe we are here to visit with your sisters, not to antagonize Forrester."

Duncan nodded and took Sinclair's advice, hurrying to his room. When he reached the top of the stairs, he glanced down to see Charlie and Sinclair in a loving embrace. He'd treated Charlie poorly and owed her an apology. He allowed his worry over Selina's welfare and her father's treatment set him on edge. Duncan responded to Charlie's good deed with the resentment he felt toward another person. Thankfully, Sinclair saw reason and ended the discussion before it flew out of control.

He continued to his room, where he found a warm bath courtesy of his mother. Also, the servants had lit a fire and set a tray of food on the nearby table. He hoped Selina received the same comforts.

~~~~~~

Lady Forrester turned Selina and ushered her up the stairs. When they reached the bedchamber, Lady Forrester hurried them inside and closed the door. The older lady bustled around, ordering Selina's maid to lay out a towel and soap for her bath. She pulled out a robe and placed it on a chair near the bathtub. Then she dismissed the maid for the afternoon, informing her she would assist Selina. After the maid left, Lady Forrester helped Selina undress down to her chemise.

Selina blushed when Lady Forrester held the dress out, and Selina saw the full impact of Duncan's destruction. His handprints weren't only covering the front of her gown but also spread across the back.

Lady Forrester smiled kindly at Selina to ease the girl's worries. "I think I shall see to the cleaning of your dress."

"I can explain." Selina twisted her hands in front of her.

Lady Forrester winked. "There is no need, my dear. 'Tis what happens when you take a fall."

Selina jumped when someone knocked on the door. Lady Forrester laid the dress across a chair and patted Selina's hand before opening the door. She took a tray from a maid. After the servant left, Lady Forrester set the tray down and poured Selina a cup of tea. She motioned for Selina to take a seat. After Selina settled, Lady Forrester poured herself a cup.

"I hope we have reassured your father of your absence."

Selina took a sip. "He will have forgotten by dinner. I am surprised he even noticed my absence."

Lady Forrester shook her head. "Of all times, Lucas chose today to seek your company."

Selina crinkled her brows. "Why?"

Lady Forrester shrugged. "I do not know. Only when he could not locate you, he went to your father, inquiring of your whereabouts. He also informed him of how no one had seen you since early this morning."

"Oh."

"Yes. Then I spoke with the servants, and Cook explained the basket she put together for you. Colebourne explained your visits to the tenants on his estate, and we guessed your destination. But we must keep our silence since your father does not approve. Then my Ramsay said Duncan followed you, and we knew you were safe. Only somewhere we could not inform your father about. Luck fell on your side when Charlie and Sinclair came upon you two with a believable story."

Selina did not hear a word Lady Forrester spoke after she said my Ramsay. She looked at Duncan's mother with confusion. "My Ramsay?"

Lady Forrester's face lit up. "My husband, dear. He arrived yesterday. However, the lengthy journey tired him, and he did not want anyone to know about his arrival yet. I cannot wait for you to become better acquainted with him. I know he will love you as I do."

"You love me?" Selina's confusion only grew while talking with Lady Forrester.

"Of course. Now I will leave you be, so you can take a bath. Then I order you to rest for the remainder of the afternoon. I will keep everyone away until it is time to dress for dinner."

Lady Forrester rose and bussed Selina's cheek before she swept out of the bedchamber with Selina's gown in her arms. Selina let her get away without answering the hundred questions on the tip of her tongue. Lady Forrester had been a whirlwind since she ushered Selina into her bedroom. Not giving her one chance to offer an explanation or to ask questions she needed answers to before dinner. Hopefully, the Sinclairs' explanation pacified her father, and he wouldn't question her further.

After slipping off her chemise, Selina stepped into the warm water and emerged herself up to her neck. She closed her eyes and let herself relax, breathing in the soothing scent of lavender before she processed what Lady Forrester discussed. Try as she might, Selina couldn't relax. Her mind wouldn't stop with its obsessive thoughts.

Ramsay, the older gentleman from the garden who Selina believed to be a servant, was Lord Forrester. Duncan's father. She should have known. Even though she had never met the lord, his appearance and personality resembled the gentleman who occupied her thoughts too closely. She couldn't fault Ramsay for wanting to keep his arrival silent.

Then there was the matter of Lady Forrester declaring how she felt about Selina. Love? She had grown closer to the lady while they prepared for her wedding, but she never imagined Lady Forrester held such strong affection toward her. But if Selina saw what was right before her, she would have seen how the lady treated her as a mother would by offering advice, complimenting her, and urging her to follow her own happiness. Lady Forrester made Selina feel loved.

It was then Selina realized the affection she held for Lady Forrester was indeed love. A giddy smile spread across Selina's face. Today, she'd gained a mother figure and realized she had friends all along.

Though, why had Charlie come to her defense? It was the perfect opportunity for her to seek revenge against Selina. Instead, she'd covered for her as a friend would. Which was as far from the truth as the lie Charlie concocted. Which begged the question: *Why?* But she understood how Charlie's mind worked and knew Charlie would make her demands soon. Selina only hoped she could comply with Lucas's conniving cousin.

Which only left her to ponder one other comment Lady Forrester spoke. Why would Gray seek her company? Was he attempting to spend time with her before they spoke their vows? Or did he wish to persuade her to break the betrothal? She knew he would refuse to break it. However, there was a clause that stated Gray or Selina could bow out of the engagement with no damages toward either party. It was an agreement she had no control over. Her father would never allow her to back out on becoming Lady Gray. So it was pointless, if that was Gray's intention. If not, then Gray would seek her out again soon.

Selina rolled over in the water and propped her chin on the edge of the tub, pondering what really had her stumbling. Why had Duncan not attempted any form of seduction today? While her heart warmed at his show of friendship, he still didn't pressure her to fall victim to his charms. Charms that became harder to resist. Charms she no longer wanted to resist. Charms he didn't display in any form other than a teasing friend who offered a warm shoulder to lay her head upon while pouring her heart out to him. However, his gaze when she'd exited the carriage spoke otherwise. She recognized the longing and knew he wanted her as deeply as she wanted him.

Her attention landed on his suit coat across her bed. It lay there, tempting Selina to return it to Duncan and find out what his desires were. Did he want her as a friend or a lover? Her need to discover the truth caused her to rise quickly from the tub, spilling water all over the floor. She didn't even bother with a towel, but wrapped her silk robe around her dripping body. She scooped the coat off the bed and rushed toward the door. Selina gasped when she turned the doorknob. She couldn't walk the length of the hallway to Duncan's bedchamber without risking someone seeing her.

She dropped her hand and leaned back against the door. She brought her fingers to her mouth and bit her nails, thinking of how to sneak into Duncan's room. Her eyes flitted around the bedroom, her breath quickening when her gaze landed on the mirror.

Of course. The secret passageway.

Why hadn't she attempted this route first? Probably because she hadn't had the nerve to wander through them before now. She only held knowledge of the passageway because Colebourne wanted her to use them for safety. He wanted her to use them if she wished to visit the library in the middle of the night, instead of opening herself to the vulnerabilities in the hallways. Also, he informed her, because she would become a member of his family, it was only right she knew of their usage.

Selina pressed the button hidden behind the mirror, and it slowly swung open. She poked her head out to see if anyone else wandered in the passageway. When she saw it empty, she stepped out and closed the secret door. Sunlight streamed in from the windows Colebourne had installed. She used the light to guide her, counting the doors along the way. When she reached the room belonging to Duncan, she paused. Her heart raced from her ragged nerves. Before she talked herself out of seeing Duncan, she pressed the latch to open his secret door. It swung open only a few inches. She stood silently, waiting for Duncan to react. When no one came near the opening, Selina peered around, looking inside the room.

She scanned the bedchamber and saw the fireplace lit. A tub filled with water stood nearby. The steam billowing above the tub indicated it was too hot to bathe in. Her gaze continued until it landed on the reason for her visit. Duncan stood just inside his room, discarding his clothing. One piece at a time, with no rush. Selina watched him unnoticed from the secret passageway. The rain had curled his long dark hair at the ends. The damp material of his shirt clung to his body as he peeled it over his head.

While he had stripped off his shirt earlier in her presence, it held more of an impact from the glow of the fire. Each ridge looked more defined. His chest and shoulders stood broader. He sat in a chair and pulled off his boots, tossing them across the room. Selina jumped when they landed near her. She stood rigid, afraid he had seen her. But when he walked over and tested the water, she realized he was still unaware of her.

He stretched, and the material of his trousers showed every aspect of his well-formed physique. It molded around his muscular thighs and emphasized how manly Duncan Forrester actually was. It left no doubt for Selina's imagination, only drawing forth a need to see him without his trousers on. He undid the placket of them, causing Selina to step forward without being aware of her actions.

She clutched his suit coat and smelled the cologne, flooding her senses with his scent. When he peeled his trousers low and tugged them off, she tried to stay silent but couldn't stop the gasp from escaping from her lips. Selina's gaze slowly traveled its way up Duncan's body, taking in every delicious inch of him. Her path lingered on his hardness, watching it grow more aroused under her bold stare.

Selina continued higher until she encountered Duncan's heated gaze drinking her in. She gulped at the desire tempting her to follow through with her plans to seduce him. Was seduction her reason for coming to his bedchamber? Yes, Selina finally confessed.

She wanted Duncan more than she needed to breathe.

Chapter Twelve

Duncan raised his head when he heard a gasp. He spun toward the door, expecting a maid to have accidentally walked in on him. He swiveled toward the secret opening when the door leading to the hallway remained closed. His gaze came upon Selina standing there, clutching his coat and raking his body with a bold stare. His heart stopped beating. When her gaze raised to meet his, it started beating again in a race to conquer Selina's heart.

As Selina's footsteps drew her closer, Duncan drank her in. Droplets of water dripped from the strands of her hair draping down her chest. The robe she wore clung to her body, damp in wetness. His gaze traveled lower, noticing her legs were bare. When she fidgeted, her robe opened to his pleasure, confirming Selina was naked. He froze. Every decision he made today in his pursuit of Selina changed with her arrival.

He refused to resist this opportunity to show Selina their destiny. Fate didn't offer him a chance like this without a reason. Duncan might be a gentleman with firm beliefs, but he was also a gentleman who couldn't resist temptation. And Selina, standing before him now, was a temptation he would risk everything for. Even if she only granted him this one chance and no other.

The pull of his gaze drew Selina to Duncan. He kept his hands to his sides, not wanting to scare her away with his need. She may have come to him, but he still noticed her indecision. There would be no return for them once they crossed over this forbidden line. They would open themselves to a vulnerability neither of them had known before. One that, if discovered, could shatter their very future.

Selina warmed at his penetrating stare. His unabashed display caused her words to stumble. "I came to return your coat." Selina held out the garment.

Duncan cocked an eyebrow. "Is that your only reason for sneaking into my bedchamber?"

Selina gulped. "Yes?"

Duncan's smile grew at her uneasiness. "Are you asking me your answer?"

Selina closed her eyes, shaking her head, then opened them again. "No."

"No, as in yes, you snuck into my bedchamber for another reason?"

Selina nodded. "I… um…" Her gaze swung to the secret opening, not sure of her motives any longer. As he stood naked before her, her nerves unraveled.

Duncan followed Selina's gaze and cursed to himself. He needed to close the door without Selina feeling trapped in his room. But the longer the door stayed ajar, the more of a risk they ran if anyone noticed them alone with Selina scantily dressed.

Duncan laid his hand on Selina's arm in a friendly gesture. "Do not feel alarmed. I am only locking both doors so no one can come upon us. I only wish to protect you. All right?"

Selina nodded, clutching his coat closer. Duncan grabbed a towel off the chair near the tub and wrapped it around his waist. He closed the secret door and secured the latch to lock it from any unwelcome visitors, for he wouldn't put it past Charlie to appear. That would give her further ammunition to destroy Selina. He then locked the bedroom door and propped a chair underneath the doorknob for more protection. Duncan returned to Selina, tugged the coat from her tight grip, and threw the coat off to the side before pulling her into his arms.

When Duncan drew Selina into his arms, every last doubt fled. His powerful arms holding her like a fragile gem gave her the security she desired. She knew in her heart that, no matter where their time led them, Duncan would protect her. His very action of locking the doors displayed his thoughtfulness.

"Can I kiss you?" he whispered.

Selina's face lit up with a seductive smile. "Ah, now the Scottish barbarian has the manners of an English gentleman."

Duncan expected shyness, not the sassiness from earlier. He growled. "Ah, I see my lady still has her claws."

Selina laughed playfully. "And if I do? May I use them upon you?"

Duncan's gaze darkened. "With pleasure," he whispered before he stole Selina's breath away.

His very kiss consumed Selina with a need so powerful, she clutched his head. Her fingers tightened in his hair with the need of keeping him anchored to her. His tongue invaded her mouth and stroked along hers in a sensual dance of longing. With each stroke, Duncan eased her yearning and replaced it with the need to explore the depth of their passion.

"Selina, Selina, Selina." Duncan groaned his need.

He pulled away from their kiss and rested his forehead against hers, staring deeply into her eyes. Their breath mingled while their eyes never broke contact. He couldn't believe her gaze held the answer to his unspoken question. However, his doubt made him hesitate from continuing with this madness.

"Love me, Duncan," Selina pleaded.

Duncan closed his eyes, fighting with what remained of his control. When Selina pressed her finger against his lips and traced them, another chunk fell. Her feather-soft touch caressed his cheek, and she softly pressed her lips to the corner of his mouth. A few more chunks dropped. Then she lifted his hand and placed it on the belt of her robe and intertwined their fingers together. He stared down at their joined hands. The symbol tumbled his defenses down around them.

Selina knew Duncan fought to act like a gentleman. For a long time, she'd fought the attraction between them, but no longer would she deny what destiny demanded from them. By giving him a sign of her surrender, she also gave herself permission to find happiness.

Duncan's fingers moved under hers, untying the knot of her robe. When the ribbon fell to the side, he took their fingers and drew them up over her stomach, over her breasts, to her bare skin. He moved them back and forth, caressing the soft skin. Selina's body reacted to Duncan's caress. Her breasts grew heavy, and her nipples scraped against the soft fabric. Her body started to tingle, and she ached for him to ease the sensations consuming her.

Duncan heard the hitch in Selina's breathing and knew she grew aroused at the gentle caress of their hands on her body. His duchess responded to her own touch. Oh, he would enjoy teaching her the fulfillment of exploring what the other found pleasure in. He brought their hands to his lips and kissed each of her fingers before placing it on his chest. Her fingers glided across his skin, exploring with no hesitancy. He groaned at her exquisite touch and knew he was a doomed man.

Duncan lowered his hands to the top of her robe and slowly slid the garment apart, drinking in her perfection. He longed to worship at her feet. There were no words to adequately describe the goddess before him. Her hair hung to her breasts, and the strands brushed back and forth across her nipples with each deep breath she drew. The buds grew tighter under his regard. He lowered his head and drew one in his mouth, savoring the sweetness. She smelled of lavender and fresh air. His tongue circled around as he gently sucked. Selina's fingers dug into his chest, extracting the claws he had given her permission to use.

His gaze lowered as he loved her breasts, and his hand stroked across her smooth stomach, dipping lower to her curls. His fingers slid into her wetness, and her dew glistened when he pulled his fingers away. At her whimper, he slid them back, drawing forth more whimpers with each stroke. His need to savor her sweetness overcame him. He dropped to his knees, ripping the garment away on his descent.

Selina's gaze widened. What was Duncan's intention? One minute, his mouth and fingers hypnotized her into holding on for dear life with his slow torture. The next, he dropped before her, and his tongue continued with the sweet torture, only more brutal than before. Fire consumed her, and each flame licked higher with each stroke of his tongue. His hand found hers and gripped it while his mouth plundered away at an ache, shaking her very core.

"Duncan." Selina's throaty moan echoed around them. She heard the need in her voice and wanted to cry at the passion clawing for release.

Her other hand gripped his head, holding him close as her body ripped itself from its tight hold. Her legs collapsed, and Duncan caught her, rising like a god from the depth of an unknown universe. He captured her lips and kissed her like a man who was on his last breath.

Each stroke of his tongue demanded that she return his need. Each brush of his lips across hers built the ache again. Each breath passed between them sealed their souls as one.

The sweet flavor of Selina on his lips enflamed his senses. But when he devoured the tantalizing nectar of the sweetest fruit, he knew this one time would never satisfy him. No. Until he conquered her heart and soul, he would never relent. Duncan refused to stop his mission of riding away in the sunset with her and living happily ever after.

He carried Selina to the tub and stepped in, lowering them into the lukewarm water. Selina settled on top of him, and he stroked her body, drawing forth more of her whimpers. It was music to his ears. Selina clutched him, her hands stroking the flames in his soul with each caress. He knew her ache grew again when each caress grew bolder. When he pressed up into her, she gasped, her eyes opening wide.

His hands lowered, and he slid a finger inside her. Her eyes closed, and her moan tickled across their tongues. Selina wanted to thrash around from the desire he brought forth, but each movement only intensified the need consuming her. Soon Duncan wrapped his arm around her waist and rolled over. Selina lay under him, vulnerable. His eyes raked her form, not leaving one spot of her untouched. The desire she saw kept her from shielding herself.

"You are a goddess sent to strike me with your beauty."

"Duncan," Selina moaned.

"Yes, my love?" Duncan traced her beauty with his hand, caressing every silken inch.

Pebbles of water clung to her nipples. His head dipped to tease them with his tongue, causing Selina to writhe around, sending water splashing onto the floor.

Selina had yet to answer him. Her moans drove him to seduce her with his carnal acts. When he pushed his fingers in deeper, she pressed up into his touch, her body arching out of the water. He sucked harder on her nipple, and her claws dug into his shoulder. His hands stroked down the length of her legs, and he drew them around his waist. He centered himself and slowly slid inside her.

Selina gasped. "Duncan?"

Duncan paused at her questioning tone. Her body tensed under his. He started to pull out, but her legs clamped around his waist, stopping him. She shook her head back and forth across the tub, her eyes heavy with desire.

"Does it hurt?" She nodded. "I need you to relax your legs, my love, so I can stop."

Selina shook her head. "But my body aches for you. It is crying for you to make me yours. It needs your soul to join with mine to survive."

Duncan shuddered at her declaration. His body shook from the need in his soul to make them one. "Do not take your eyes from mine," he ordered.

Selina's gaze clung to his as he pressed deeper inside her, each movement slower than the last. When he pushed past her barrier, Selina sighed and melted in his arms. He fought the need to drive into her over and over. Her whimpered moans stabbed at his desire to stake his claim.

Selina sank deeper into the water at the sheer pleasure of Duncan inside her. His fullness heightened her desire to have him take her with a driving force of need. He held himself still, and Selina watched him fight with his inner urges to be gentle with her. However, their passion wouldn't stay contained. To experience the full impact, she needed Duncan to unleash his control.

She pressed her hips against his, and he shook against her. He growled when she scraped her nails down his back. Selina slid her legs up and down his, and then tightened them around his waist again.

It wasn't until she whispered, "Make me yours," that Duncan lost the remains of his control.

Her whisper was his undoing. He took possession of Selina's body with hard, firm strokes. Each one driving in deeper than the last. Each time, her moans fueled their passion higher. Selina molded herself around him, holding onto him. He grabbed her waist to keep her from sinking under the water as he drove them to the highest filling of ecstasy one could journey to.

Selina found herself rapidly falling until Duncan caught her in his arms, and she floated with him. One moment Duncan was above her, making love to her, then she exploded in his arms. Now she lay curled in his embrace, with his hands stroking through her hair and murmuring tender affections in her ear. While his touch was gentle and his body relaxed under hers, his heart still thudded. The sound comforted her.

Duncan smiled when Selina traced the droplets across his chest. His duchess had finally recovered. She rolled over and raised her gaze. He expected to see a blush or a glimpse of regret. However, her eyes blazed with the same need as his. His cock grew hard. He would be a brute to make love to her again so soon.

Duncan growled, lowering his head and kissing her hard. "Stop staring at me like that."

"Like what?" Selina's husky voice shivered along his spine.

Duncan shook his head, refusing to answer. She only provoked him with a temptation he struggled to resist. When her hand wandered lower, he grabbed it and brought it to his lips.

"Do you not find pleasure from my touch?" Selina pouted.

Duncan gritted his teeth, fighting his body's urges. If she touched him now, he couldn't control himself. Then he would never forgive himself for hurting her. Selina may feel a high from their lovemaking, but her body would feel a tenderness. He grabbed a washcloth and soap. Duncan washed Selina, taking extra care between her thighs. When she winced, her pain shot through him. He gave her a gentle kiss on the lips.

"I find much pleasure from your touch. But I refuse to show you how much of a barbarian I can be."

Selina's mouth dropped open in understanding. "Oh."

Duncan chuckled. "Yes. Oh."

Selina nestled her head under his neck, her face brightening to a becoming shade of pink. He groaned when the blush consumed her body. He needed out of this tub and her wrapped back into her robe. Or he wouldn't hold himself responsible for his actions. Duncan could only resist so much before he gave in to his desires.

And Selina Pemberton was one desire he would never get enough of.

He stood and stepped out of the tub, carrying Selina to a chair before the fire. Duncan grabbed the towel he'd discarded earlier and dried her off, wrapping her in a blanket while he dried himself. Once he finished, he held out his hand, and she slipped her hand into his trustingly. He led them to his bed, lifting her up and laying her in the middle. Then he crawled in next to her, pulling the covers over them.

The rain continued to fall, harder from when they arrived back at the manor. It was the type of day to laze around in bed. He knew no one would disturb them, and hopefully, their absence would go unnoticed. Duncan wanted to hold Selina in his arms before she must return to her room. He feared once he let her go, their connection would become severed. If it did, Duncan didn't know how he would survive without her.

"I should return," Selina said, covering a yawn with her hand.

"Let me hold you for a while longer. I will make sure you return before your maid comes to dress you for dinner."

Selina snuggled into him. "Just for a few more minutes."

Neither one of them spoke of the line they'd crossed this afternoon. Neither one of them wanted to ruin the special moment or confront the guilt weighing on their conscience.

They only wished to absorb the embrace of their love.

Chapter Thirteen

Selina's thoughts drifted while Lady Forrester discussed the flower arrangements for the wedding brunch. The lady didn't need Selina's input, but would have appreciated it nonetheless. However, ever since Selina and Duncan made love, Selina hadn't been able to concentrate on a single conversation. Luckily for her, not many people tried to engage with her. Over the years, she had perfected how to show interest in her father's discussions. So whenever he confronted her, Selina kept a serene expression on her face and agreed to his demands.

Which only left a small circle of people who sought her company. They were always polite and tried to engage her with small talk. Lucas and his cousins, as usual, avoided her at all costs. But their rejection no longer stung as it had before. Perhaps because she found comfort in her friendship with Anna and the other villagers.

To be honest, Lady Forrester treated Selina differently. Her gestures turned loving, and she would occasionally wrap Selina in a hug. Selina even found Lady Forrester gazing fondly at her with a mysterious smile upon her face. She showed extreme patience with Selina's distraction.

Then there was Ramsay. He refused for her to call him Lord Forrester. He muttered something to the effect that the proper behavior of the gentry was pure bollocks. To cover his salty language, he apologized for his deception in keeping his identity a secret from her. He meant no harm, but he'd wanted to avoid the proper decorum his arrival would prompt. Selina forgave him and since then had shared many walks in the garden with him. He'd even joined her for a ride this morning, showing her a few spots she hadn't noticed before.

Although her stay might have turned enjoyable, it also brought forth more quandaries for Selina. Her major dilemma was in the form of one very unforgettable Scotsman. A gentleman who was the source of her mind's wanderings, a most tantalizing source who kept wrapping her in a warm embrace of love. When she awoke at dawn, a rose rested on the pillow next to her with a message. A blush warmed Selina's cheek while she recalled Duncan's scandalous words.

S,

The fragrance of this rose reminds me of the fragrance of our love.
Your devoted lover,

D

Selina had scrambled to hide the rose and letter when her maid bustled in to help her dress. Selina pressed the rose in her book of poems and kept the letter by her side. Throughout the day, when no one else was nearby, she withdrew the letter to read again. She itched to devour the intensity of his words even now.

It had been two days since they spent the afternoon in each other's arms. Two days and Selina had only grown more attached to Duncan. When the time came for them to part, she feared her heart would shatter into a million pieces. She ached to lie in his arms again and feel the passion they shared. His stolen kisses weren't enough. Her body desired to join with his and escape into the magic meant for them alone.

"Selina? Selina?" Lady Forrester's voice broke through Selina's musings.

Startled, Selina shook her head to clear her thoughts. "I apologize, Lady Forrester. I am afraid my thoughts have taken me elsewhere."

"No need, my dear. I understand. The closer your wedding day draws near, the more your mind can become distracted."

Selina nodded. "Yes, my wedding day. Exactly, Lady Forrester."

Selina held no clue on what she agreed to about her wedding day. Shame overcame her. She didn't think of her wedding at all but the lady's son instead. What would Lady Forrester think of her carousing with her son while planning Selina's wedding to her nephew? Selina fought against the shame that hovered on her conscience. She refused to allow guilt to seep in for stealing precious memories of happiness before she committed to a life of loneliness.

Lady Forrester moved to sit next to Selina on the settee. "Selina, will you please call me Susanna? I feel we have grown closer over the last few weeks. I do not wish to replace a mother in your eyes, but I feel a motherly affection toward you."

Tears came to Selina's eyes. "You are too kind to me."

Lady Forrester chuckled. "Nonsense."

"I thank you for your offer, Susanna. I feel honored at your regard."

"Honored enough to confide your troubles? I only ask because they seem to occupy your thoughts heavily. I wish for your input on your wedding and the reception to follow, yet you have none. It is not my intention to force my ideas on your memorable day."

Selina smiled wistfully. "To be honest, I have no care how the day plays itself out. The outcome will end the same, regardless."

Susanna smiled encouragingly. "Then humor me. If your wedding day were upon us and you looked upon the ceremony with anticipation, how would it proceed?"

Selina thought about how she wished for her wedding day to happen. It was foolish to engage in such fantasies, but Lady Forrester's eagerness prompted Selina to divulge her dream wedding.

"It would be a modest affair with no grand show. I only want the ones who love us present with a few close friends invited. An exchanging of vows in the village church. I would wear the dress we've chosen, of course. It is too exquisite not to." Selina paused, remembering Duncan's appreciation of the dress. "Then for the celebration, a grand picnic with simple fare, music, and dancing. Not the formal dances everyone expects of a duke's son marrying a duke's daughter, but ones of carefree abandonment. I only wish for a merry affair."

Lady Forrester's face lit up with fascination. "And how do you picture the groom by your side?"

Selina bit her bottom lip, tears coming forth to her eyes again. "Excuse me, Lady Forrester. I fear I have gotten something in my eye."

"Selina?"

Selina rose and scurried from the room, not stopping when Lady Forrester called out. With her head bent, she didn't see the gentlemen standing in the doorway until she collided with them. She gasped and took a step back, stepping into a curtsy.

"Your Grace, and Lord Forrester, I must apologize."

Lord Forrester stepped forward, grabbing a hold of Selina's hand and winking at her. "Lord Forrester? Why the formality, my dear? Remember, I have requested for you to call me Ramsay."

Selina attempted a smile. "I remember. Please accept my apologies for leaving so swiftly. I promised my father to meet him."

Colebourne smiled warmly. "Of course, my dear. You will find your father in the library."

She nodded before taking her leave. Selina needed to put distance between her and Lady Forrester before she spilled about how her ideal groom wasn't her intended. Instead, the lady's son was who Selina pictured as her groom.

Colebourne watched Selina scurry away in the opposite direction of the library and chuckled at Susanna. "What did you say to the poor girl?"

Susanna cackled. "Why, I only inquired how she pictured her wedding day and the groom by her side."

Ramsay shook his head at their machinations before sitting down next to his wife. "From the girl's expression, one would think you were tormenting her."

"And how does Lady Selina picture her wedding day?" asked Colebourne

"A simple affair with family and friends."

Colebourne pinched his lips. "Would it take too much to alter the wedding you have already planned?"

Susanna shook her head with excitement. "'Tis no trouble at all. In fact, her ideal wedding is much like our Scottish affairs."

Ramsay chuckled. "Now this wedding I would not mind attending."

Colebourne narrowed his gaze. "And her ideal groom?"

Susanna sighed. "That is where I am afraid I lost her confidence, and she fled."

Colebourne started pacing back and forth across the room. "I thought Duncan's pursual of Selina would have progressed further. He is running out of time to win her hand. What is the delay?"

Susanna sighed. "I thought perhaps it had proceeded. The past two days, Selina has not focused on our discussions. She sits before me with a dreamy expression. Not to mention the lingering glances between her and Duncan. I even spotted my son stealing a kiss from Selina when he thought no one watched."

Ramsay growled. "You two cannot force a love affair."

Susanna laid a hand on her husband's arm. "We are not forcing anything, my love. But only guiding them toward a lifetime they both wish for."

Ramsay swung his gaze toward Colebourne. "Now you have convinced my wife to follow you on this path of madness. A destination that will end with heartache for all the souls involved. You call it guiding when truly it is a kind term for conspiring. Perhaps you two should stop trying to force fate and allow it to proceed on its own terms."

"Scottish rubbish," Colebourne muttered.

"Well, it is better than English bollocks," Ramsay muttered in return.

Susanna chuckled at their insults. "Gentlemen, behave. Now, Ramsay, you promised to help bring them together. Why the sudden change of heart?"

"Because I spend much time in the lass's company, and I see the sadness lurking in her eyes when she thinks no one watches her. I also see the longing and guilt in my son's gaze. By throwing them together at every opportunity, you are only compounding the misery of their union. And I, for one, want no part of it." Ramsay stood, looking down upon his wife. "Nor will I stand in your way. I only wish to hear no more of this matchmaking madness." Ramsay nodded at Colebourne and left the parlor.

Colebourne sighed, sitting next to Susanna. "I am sorry, my dear. I should not have involved you in this debacle."

Susanna laughed and clapped her hands. "Oh, this is perfect."

Colebourne looked at her with confusion. "How so?"

Susanna relaxed back against the cushion. "We could not have asked for a better outcome. With Ramsay's objection toward us, it will only prompt him to discuss the improper pursuit of Selina with Duncan. Ramsay will voice all of his reasons for Duncan to halt his intentions. Which will only push Duncan to defy his father as he has always done when faced with his father's disapproval." Susanna rolled her eyes. "He always has to prove his father wrong."

Colebourne leaned back too and chuckled. "Ah, I think you may be even more devious than me. Let us hope your plan works, for our time is closing in."

Susanna nodded. "All we have left is hope."

Chapter Fourteen

Duncan watched Selina bolt from the parlor his father and uncle had just entered. He had waited in the shadows for his mother and Selina to finish their conversation, gritting his teeth. His mother had gushed over the details of Selina's wedding day, sharing her delight at the flowers she'd arranged for the ceremony. When he snuck a peek inside the parlor, Selina hadn't been paying attention to his mother, but sat wearing a dreamy expression, lost in thought.

Did her attention stray in the same manner Duncan's had in the past two days? He couldn't forget the memory of Selina's expression of ecstasy when he made love to her. He ached to steal another kiss, and it was the perfect moment to do so. Duncan kept a few paces behind her as she snuck inside a small parlor that wasn't used much because of its size.

Uncle Theo had designed the parlor for his wife shortly after they were wed. The parlor was where Uncle Theo, Aunt Olivia, and Lucas had spent many nights together. Duncan had discovered that Selina escaped to this room whenever something troubled her. Abigail used the parlor quite often, too. How the two never crossed paths amazed him. Since Abigail was visiting with his other cousins on the terrace, no one would disturb them, least of all Lucas. His cousin kept his distance from Selina.

Duncan eased the door open and found Selina reading a letter. Her distraction was to his advantage. He closed the door and walked to the settee, leaning over her shoulder. He whispered in her ear, "What are you reading, my love, that has taken over your attention?"

Selina gasped, turning in her seat.

Duncan chuckled and wanted to kiss the surprise from her face. It would appear his duchess carried his letter with her and stole a glance at it again.

Selina stuffed the letter back into her pocket, pulling away and putting some much-needed distance between them. She didn't answer and wanted to leave before he discovered her discomfort.

Selina withdrew from him, and he wondered about her sudden change of behavior. Whenever their paths crossed, she had welcomed his flirtation, even displaying her own affection toward him. Dinner the previous evening was proof of how their bond only strengthened. She had placed her hand on this thigh and drawn small circles with her fingers, bringing him to the brink of voicing his love for her aloud. When his breath hitched at her bold display, she pulled her hand away, only for Duncan to grab ahold and link their hands together. When she didn't pull away and sat with a charming smile upon her lips at the pleasure, he stared at her like a lovesick fool throughout dinner.

He only had to suffer from Charlie's teasing later, but his cousin stopped once she realized she couldn't faze him. He only smiled and agreed with everything she said, which only riled Charlie. For Duncan's safety, Sinclair pulled his wife away before she retaliated.

Duncan rounded the settee and sat next to Selina, pulling her hand into his grasp. "What is the matter?"

Selina wiped a tear away before Duncan noticed. "Nothing. I am only feeling sentimental."

Duncan frowned. "For what?"

Selina attempted a smile. "For a lady I never knew and one I wished was here. I am afraid my imagination has carried itself away in its creation."

"I am confused."

"My mother. My wedding day draws near, and I wish for her guidance. Your mother kindly offered her support, and not that I do not appreciate her. I only …"

Duncan drew Selina into his arms. "I understand, and I am sure my mother does too." He tipped Selina's face up to him. "You have charmed my mother, my dear. Not to mention my father too."

Selina softened in Duncan's arms. "They are dear people."

He chuckled. "A kind way to describe them."

She smiled.

"I am sorry you have missed out on the experience of a mother, and I wish I had the magical ability to grant you one."

She slid her palm over his cheek. "You get your kindness from them."

His smile turned mischievous. "Not too long ago you declared your pity for them for having a son like me."

"Oh, I still hold pity for them," Selina teased.

Duncan stared in awe at the twinkling amusement in Selina's eyes. One moment, tears filled them. Now they reflected how comfortable she felt in teasing him. While he could stare into her eyes all day, he longed for desire to fill them again, to place his lips against her and watch the fire flame to life. The connection would cloud both of their judgments with an uncontrollable passion.

Duncan's gaze changed from amusement to the sinful delight of passion. She knew with one touch of his lips on hers, her own desires would ignite. To be honest, his very nearness built her need to an unbearable ache only his kiss would help to ease.

Duncan leaned in closer. "Selina?"

Her lids grew heavy. "Mmm?"

He drew his hand to the back of her neck and arched her head, then trailed his thumb across her bottom lip. "I am going to kiss you."

Selina sighed. "Please do."

Duncan needed no other encouragement. He bent his head and kissed Selina with a slowness, stopping time. Each pull of his lips against hers savored the temptation. Each sigh was captured and drawn into each other's souls. Each stroke of their tongues fueled the passion their bodies craved.

This was unlike any kiss they'd shared before. It held desperation to it like no other. Selina clutched him with a fierceness he didn't understand, but one he needed to reassure her with. However, he knew she would refuse to hear his stand on their relationship. So, he did what he knew best. He lived in the moment of their kiss, hoping Selina would see reason and profess her love. They could overcome any scandal associated with their union together.

Selina deepened the kiss, trying to ease the anguish consuming her. Too many factors clouded her judgment. She felt trapped in her situation, and with each kiss from Duncan, the chains only wrapped tighter. She sank her fingers into his thick waves and clung to his lips. Her desperation to have her upcoming wedding disappear made her crave Duncan's soft touch. His whispered words of affection, his slow, drugging kisses, his body joining hers in the sweetest rapture.

"Duncan?"

Duncan's kiss changed when Selina whispered his name. He couldn't handle it if she were to ask him to stop. While Selina had kissed him fervently, his kiss soon matched hers.

Selina pulled away. "Duncan?" Her tone was firmer.

Duncan growled his frustration. "What?"

"I need you to love me." The same desperation in her kisses filled Selina's gaze.

Duncan sighed in relief. "With pleasure."

He rose and pulled Selina after him. He paused, glancing at the bookcase and the door. Duncan wished to sneak Selina through the secret passageway to his bedroom. However, if someone had seen them both enter the parlor, they would expect them to depart from there. He didn't want to risk any suspicion on either of their reputations. They risked too much as it was for their affair. Uncle Theo kept a relaxed household where the servants never questioned if an unmarried lady kept company with a gentleman. Even though Selina's father felt differently, with her marriage to Lucas taking place next week, he would assume her virtue remained intact.

They separated quickly when raised voices from the hallway led to the door flying open. Before Lucas and Abigail spotted them, Selina sat on a chair, and Duncan turned toward the bookcase, pulling out a book.

"Here is the book I was telling you about." Duncan handed it to Selina, pretending their visit was innocent in nature. "Oh, Lucas and Abigail, how pleasant of you to join us."

Lucas stopped in his tracks, his gaze narrowing while he glanced back and forth between Duncan and Selina. His stare landed on Selina, and he growled, "Why are you in this room?"

Selina jerked back at the harshness of Lucas's tone. He only ever talked to her in this manner when she had done something upsetting to

Abigail or one of his cousins. Since she had shown no cruelty since her arrival, she grew confused about why Lucas would strike at her. "I, ahh... That is..."

Duncan's hands curled into fists at his side, and he tried to rein in his fury, not wanting to draw any more suspicion upon them. However, Lucas's behavior toward Selina was unforgivable. "I noticed Lady Selina spending her time alone, with no one offering to visit with her. So, I convinced her to join me in your mother's favorite parlor. I explained to her the special meaning of the room since she is soon to call Colebourne Manor her home. Over the course of our discussion, I mentioned a book I thought she might enjoy reading. If there is any fault for her presence in this room, the fault lies with me."

Abigail stepped forward, wearing a false smile. "I am sure Lucas meant no harm. And you stand correct, Duncan. Soon Lady Selina will be mistress of Colebourne Manor, and she should have every room available for her access." Abigail directed her words at Lucas with emphasis, declaring what everyone in the parlor tried to forget.

Selina rose and rushed to the door. When she reached the entryway, she turned. "Thank you, Lord Forrester. I shall retire to my room for the afternoon to read this treasure you have spoken so highly of. Good day." She nodded to Abigail and Lucas.

Duncan watched Selina's face pale at her polite retreat. He waited for her footsteps to fade before he unleashed his fury at his cousin. "You uncaring bastard, how could you be so heartless to her?"

Lucas rolled his eyes. "Please, as if she did not deserve it. She has laid her own viciousness at our feet for years."

Duncan gritted his teeth. "Are you not only cruel, but blind too? Have you not seen her change of behavior since her arrival?"

Lucas scoffed. "'Tis only an act to fool my father. Norbury and Lady Selina realize Father wants out of the betrothal agreement, and they are trying everything in their power to change her image."

"You are a bloody fool!" Duncan shouted. "She is not the person you imagine her to be."

Lucas pierced Duncan with his stare. "And pray tell, cousin, how do you view Lady Selina? I only wonder because I found you alone with her, and you are swift to defend her honor."

Both men glared, moving to within an inch of each other. "Perhaps if *you* spent time with her, *you* would be the one defending her honor. Are you feeling the restraint of your impending marital vows?"

"However I choose to treat Lady Selina is of no concern of yours. Especially once she becomes my wife!" Lucas snarled.

Abigail gasped at the mention of Selina becoming Lucas's wife. Another victim in this madness. Both of the gentlemen had forgotten her in their argument. Her lips trembled in distress. Duncan backed away from Lucas, drawing his hand through his hair. He didn't mean to upset Abigail in his defense of Selina. But his cousin's callous disregard for the woman Duncan loved infuriated him.

"Abigail," Lucas called out when Abigail ran from the room.

Lucas attempted to chase after her, but Duncan reached out and stopped him. "Leave her be. You have caused enough damage for one afternoon."

Lucas shook off Duncan's hold, rounding on him. His eyes blazed with fury, and Duncan stood still, waiting for him to unleash his frustration.

But before their argument rose to the next level, Colebourne interrupted them.

"For once, your cousin stands correct, Lucas. However, both of your actions with two unmarried ladies in my household arouses my suspicion. I have decided how I will handle this behavior. If you will follow me to my study, we can discuss this in private." Colebourne turned on his heel and strode away, expecting them to follow.

Duncan and Lucas snarled at each other before following Colebourne. If any servants had heard their argument, they had made themselves scarce. The manor held an eerie silence. While Colebourne never raised his voice, his disappointment rang clear. Whatever decision he'd made, it wouldn't be to either his or Lucas's liking. Also, he feared how it would relate to Selina. The stolen moments he wished to share with her now hung in the balance of being ripped away. All because he couldn't control his temper. He wished he possessed his father's ability to remain calm during a confrontation.

Colebourne rounded his desk and sat in his chair. He leaned forward, regarding his son and nephew. He shook his head in exasperation. For men who were maturing into two highly intelligent lads, they were both complete fools. Colebourne had hoped Duncan's infatuation with Selina would have prompted him to wear her defenses down enough for her to withdraw from the betrothal. Instead, he moved at a snail's pace to convince her of his love.

Then there was his son. During this time, Lucas should have attempted to discourage Selina's attention, displaying his boorish manners. Instead, he ignored her, thinking his disinterest would solve his problem. Colebourne only noticed the poor girl was racked with guilt and confusion.

Oh, he saw the affection between Duncan and Selina when they thought no one noticed. However, what his nephew failed to see was that while Selina held a dreamy expression when they were together, she also held an expression full of remorse. They both toyed with Selina's emotions. And it would end now. He would declare his orders and force them to make a move toward their happiness. He would allow them enough slack and hope they didn't hang themselves with it.

The duke pointed at the chairs. "Take a seat."

Duncan and Lucas sat across from him, anger brimming beneath the surface. He silently chuckled. Before he laid down the law, he would give them a chore to work on their frustrations. One they would have to perform together. They might hold the rank of a lord, but he never allowed them to believe they were better than the servants who worked for him.

"After we finish our discussion, you are both to report to the stables to assist Emery with the new shipment of cattle I am expecting tomorrow. I want the stables mucked and fresh hay laid out. Also, there are stalls which need repairs. I do not want to see either of you until you complete this task. Is this understood?" He pulled his cigar case closer, opening the lid.

"Yes, sir." They both spoke clearly and sat up straighter in their chairs.

Colebourne nodded before lighting a cigar. "Now from what I have gathered, you two disagree on how Lady Selina should be treated."

"Lucas treats her unfairly."

"I found Duncan alone with her."

Colebourne held up a hand for their silence. "You have a valid point, Duncan. However, so does Lucas. Your attention to Lady Selina is causing gossip and speculation on Norbury's part. I will give you one of two choices on how you wish to proceed.

Duncan gripped the chair. He knew he would dislike his uncle's choices. "And they are?"

"You may either pack your bags and return to Scotland. Or you will stay away from Lady Selina until her wedding day. Your only association will be in a polite manner. No more time spent alone unless someone else is present. Then you will show her the same regard one would expect from a distant cousin. I will discuss with your mother the seating arrangements for our meals. From this day forth, Selina will sit between Lucas and a gentleman of my choosing. So, what will your decision be, my boy?" Colebourne took a puff of his cigar, watching Duncan for any sign of a reaction.

Duncan sat as still as he could. He wouldn't allow his uncle to see how much his choices affected him. If he acted out on his frustration, it would give his uncle the ammunition he needed to attack and take the decision out of Duncan's hands. He should feel grateful for his uncle allowing him a choice. Uncle Theo could have demanded his return to Scotland. While his uncle regarded him with a shrewd gaze, Duncan realized he had thrown down this gauntlet to push Duncan into action. Uncle Theo took pleasure from Duncan's defense of Selina and goaded him.

Duncan stole a glance over at Lucas and realized his cousin held no clue on what his father planned behind his back.

No, Duncan wasn't a fool. He knew his uncle wished for Lucas and Abigail to wed. And once he saw how Duncan reacted around Selina, it gave him the idea to play his mad matchmaking schemes on them. It was the very reason for his invite to stay at his home in London and the reason for his father's appearance. His father never left their castle unless it concerned his mother or Duncan. Uncle Theo planned for Duncan to become Selina's groom, and his mother had convinced his father to visit. Why else would his father befriend Selina like he had if their marriage weren't to become the eventual outcome? So, he would continue to play along with his uncle's schemes.

"I will stay and keep my distance from Lady Selina," Duncan gritted between his teeth. He needed to stay angry, to fool his uncle, and for the benefit of Lucas. If his cousin chose to remain dense to his father's agenda, then far be it for Duncan to enlighten him. In truth, his cousin needed to suffer for his ill-treatment of Selina and Abigail.

Colebourne continued smoking his cigar. "Wise choice, my boy. Now, Lucas, we shall discuss your behavior toward Lady Selina. I have noticed your ill manners, and only this morning her father brought it to my attention how you do not speak or spend time with her. Is this true?"

Lucas stayed silent in his seat, refusing to defend himself. It wouldn't matter, anyway. His father's demands stood firm, no matter what anyone else desired. Why should he pay court to a lady his father forced him to wed? He needed to convince his father to stop Abigail from leaving. He refused to soothe the tattered emotions of a shrew he'd once considered a friend. Selina's brutal treatment toward Abigail during the season had caused him to hold Selina in the same regard as the rest of his family. Lucas thought they could form a union to pacify their parents and find a common ground of friendship, but as the day drew nearer, he realized everything he must sacrifice if he spoke his marital vows. A sacrifice of his true love. Abigail.

Colebourne tapped his ashes against the tray. "So is this how you wish for our discussion to proceed?"

Lucas narrowed his gaze at his father. "It does not matter what I say. Let us save ourselves and lay down your demands."

"Very well. After your time spent in the stables, every free minute you have, you shall become a devoted servant to Lady Selina. You will sit next to her at every meal, take walks in the garden with her, read to her, and anything else demanding your attention toward her. You will leave no doubt in her mind or her father's of our family's honor securing the promise made to them."

Lucas stood up and pressed his hands on the desk. "Father, I do not have time to court Selina, nor is there a need to. I must convince Abigail how foolish her plans are. She has accepted a position as a governess."

Colebourne stubbed out his cigar and relaxed back into his chair. "I am well aware of Abigail's plans. But if you remember correctly, I have secured a groom for Abigail. One who has accepted an invitation to your wedding to Lady Selina." Colebourne emphasized the marriage to goad his son. "Soon I shall have Abigail settled. And as I have also stated before, she is none of your concern."

"I beg to differ," Lucas growled.

Colebourne shrugged his indifference. No one had ever crossed his authority before, and his own son shall be no different. "Nevertheless, I have made my decision."

"Who is this supposed gentleman, and is he aware of your plot to trap him?"

Colebourne chuckled his amusement. "You shall meet him soon, and no, he is still unaware. I thought him a more intelligent bloke, but lately, he has proven himself not to be. Perhaps in time he shall grow wiser."

Duncan couldn't help himself and barked out a laugh at his uncle's attempt at humor on Lucas's behalf. Lucas swung an irritated glance at him before turning back to his father. "I will warn Abigail and this supposed gentleman when the time comes."

"By all means, my son. You take whatever precaution you think is best. Now you boys are due in the stables. If either of you strays from my demands, one of you will find yourself sent to Scotland while the other will find his marriage moved forward. Do I make myself clear?"

Duncan and Lucas nodded, then took their leave. One of them left seething with rage while the other walked away with the biggest grin on his face, which only led Colebourne to believe Duncan was onto his scheme. That was just the effect he hoped for. Hopefully, the boy picked up his game at a much faster rate than he'd played so far. Colebourne hoped by keeping a distance between Selina and Duncan, and pressing Lucas's company on Selina, it would compel the lady to see how her life would progress if she didn't embrace Duncan's love.

A tricky play on his part. However, sometimes one had to gamble in the game of matchmaking. You threw the dice and hoped it landed to your advantage.

Chapter Fifteen

Colebourne forced Duncan and Lucas to work alongside each other throughout the day. Each time one of them tried to work elsewhere, Emery forced them back together again. They realized they were the only ones who toiled when they broke for dinner. Upon they questioned Emery, he informed them that Colebourne had sent orders for the servants to enjoy dinner and the evening with their families. Lucas and Duncan could finish the day's work. The stable master cackled his glee and wished them luck before taking off to enjoy an evening at the village tavern.

Now they sat inside a stall, eating their dinner a servant had delivered over an hour ago. While it appeared both of their tempers had calmed, they had yet to speak. Throughout the day, they only answered each other with grunts. Duncan wanted to laugh at the absurdity of the situation. He understood Lucas's frustration with Abigail, but he didn't understand why Lucas acted territorial about Selina. Lucas had made his opinion of Selina clear, so why did he care if Duncan spent time in her company?

Duncan dug through the basket and pulled out a bottle of whiskey. "Ah, just the reward for a tiring day of punishment."

Lucas grabbed the bottle from his hands and took a long swallow. "I agree, cousin. This makes it all worthwhile for the trouble you caused."

Duncan grabbed the bottle back. "Trouble I caused? You were the one who sent two ladies away in tears."

Lucas sighed. "I owe Abigail an apology."

"And Selina?"

Lucas shook his head. "Only under the duress of my father's threats will I offer her an apology. She deserves no more. Now I am forced to have her stuck by my side until we wed. My remaining days of freedom were for me to enjoy before my marriage became a shackle I will have to endure for a lifetime."

Duncan grew irritated at how Lucas perceived his marriage to Selina would be. He needed to keep his temper calm and his opinions of Selina to himself if he were to convince Lucas of Selina's more favorable traits.

"Perhaps you should take this opportunity to learn more about Selina. Maybe under all her layers a lady with a kind heart lies."

Lucas narrowed his gaze. "Why do you defend her? If I recall, the two of you are quick to slander one another."

Duncan shrugged. "I have gotten to know her better. Since you ran after Abigail when she left London, your father forced me to escort Selina to the entertainments in your place."

"Well, we are no longer in London. You no longer need to entertain her."

Duncan took a drink. "She is a delightful companion. Quite charming when her viper tongue is not striking."

"A charming viper. What a future I have to look forward to," Lucas scoffed.

Duncan shoved Lucas backward, unseating him. "You are a lucky bastard and do not even appreciate it."

Lucas sat back up. "If you feel so strongly, then why do you not marry her?"

Duncan stood up and walked out of the stall. "It would be my honor," he muttered lowly enough that Lucas didn't hear.

He couldn't stay around his cousin any longer without pounding into him. Duncan wanted to steal into Selina's bedchamber and love her. He needed to apologize for Lucas's behavior, kiss away her heartache, and hold her close.

Then he would have to suffer, watching Lucas and Selina spend time together. If he were an uncaring bastard and she didn't mean more to him, he would have taken up his uncle's offer and fled. However, he loved her too much, and their time was slipping away for him to convince her to choose him.

He didn't make it very far when Lucas swung him around. "What did you say?"

"Nothing."

"Yes, you did."

Duncan sighed. "Why not give her a chance? Do you know she visits your tenants and reads to the young children so their mothers can take a break?"

"Selina?"

Duncan nodded.

Lucas grew silent and thought over Duncan's defense of Selina. There had been times over the years that he'd enjoyed her company while riding or talking during her brief visits. She had a more spiteful relationship with his cousins, but it had never crossed the lines of their friendship. It had only been since the start of the season when she'd turned cruel. While he had been insensitive toward her, perhaps she suffered from the same pressure as he did.

"All right. I shall offer her a chance. Tomorrow I must visit some tenants, and I will take her along."

"And you will treat her kindly. The rest of our family will not unless you do the same."

Lucas took a drink and offered the bottle to Duncan. "I will make this right. Now, shall we finish this bottle and forget about earlier?"

Duncan threw back a drink. "All is forgotten."

They returned to the stall and finished the contents in the basket, no longer discussing Selina or Abigail. There wasn't much discussion at all, only the bottle being passed back and forth in comfortable silence. Each gentleman contemplated their next course of action. One must convince his bride to break their betrothal while the other needed to steal his cousin's bride away.

The only way to achieve their outcomes was to resort to madness.

~~~~~

Selina lay in bed, facing the secret passageway, and prayed for Duncan to walk through it. She had retired early, pleading a headache. Lady Forrester had ordered a sleeping tonic to help Selina rest through her ailment. She pretended to be asleep when her maid checked in on her.

She hadn't seen Duncan since Lucas attacked her. Selina had spent the afternoon hiding in her bedroom. Her emotions flipped from suffering a deep sadness, to feeling hurt from Lucas's cruelty, to anger at not defending herself. She wondered why she tried to show her true character when no one wanted to learn who the true Selina Pemberton was. No, they would rather cling to their unforgiveness and hatefulness. Well, she would no longer allow their regard to bother her.

She learned other people enjoyed her companionship, and she had friends all along. If everyone else refused to like Selina, then she refused to please those who wouldn't accept her for who she was. She wouldn't grovel for their attention and kindness any longer. If they wanted to consider her an enemy, then it was their choice, not hers.

However, during dinner, the strong declaration she made to herself earlier caused her doubts. It'd been the usual affair, except Lucas and Duncan were absent. No one spoke about why they weren't present. Their absence must be the reason Duncan hadn't sought her company throughout the day.

The dinner was a subdued affair. Colebourne kept landing his gaze on either Selina or Abigail. He appeared deep in thought and kept nodding to himself. Lady Forrester tried to keep the conversation flowing, but the tense atmosphere flooding the room grew too thick to penetrate. Selina was positive everyone had heard of the encounter in the parlor. Lord and Lady Forrester passed her too many sympathizing glances for them not to know. Her father's glare was more brutal than usual. Even Abigail's glances struck her strangely. Any time Selina's gaze wandered the table and landed on Abigail, she offered Selina a timid smile. Some would describe the expression as pity. However, Selina believed it was a gesture of how they shared a bond, suffering from the same affliction. The misery of loving a man out of their grasp.

When Duncan still didn't show, she'd pleaded a headache and escaped to her room, where she kept waiting for him. She drank the tea, hoping it calmed her nerves. Her eyes drifted closed, and she opened them wide again, fighting against the sleep her body craved. Her emotions had wreaked havoc on her today, wearing her down emotionally. Perhaps if she closed her eyes for a brief moment, Duncan would appear once she opened them again.

~~~~~~

Duncan and Lucas stumbled up the stairs. Once they reached the landing, they knocked over a vase, shattering it across the floor. They paused at the loud breakage and then started laughing at their foolishness. Various doors opened along the hallway. Once they noticed their inebriated state, they shook their heads and closed their doors. Everyone except Jacqueline. She stormed out of her room, shaking her head in disappointment at them. Luckily for them, Colebourne, Norbury, and Duncan's parents' bedrooms were in another wing.

Duncan tilted his head at Jacqueline's attire and disheveled hair. If his judgment weren't clouded by alcohol, he would have voiced his opinion on her ravished appearance. Her lips were plump, and he thought she might be naked under her robe. He shook his head. He must be drunker than he thought. His eyes grew heavy as he tried to concentrate on her scolding.

"You two have caused more than enough trouble today. Can you not retire to your rooms in silence? Why must you disturb our sleep because of your callous disregard?"

Duncan looked at her with one eye closed. "Sleeping, were ye?" He took a step toward her bedroom.

A pinkness stole over her cheeks, and she pressed herself against the door. "Yes. Why else would I be about at this late hour?"

Lucas chuckled behind him. Duncan joined in with his laughter and waggled his eyebrows. "Only trouble."

She clutched her robe tighter, watching Lucas pass them on his way to Abigail's room. "Lucas, get away from there," she hissed.

"I only wish to apologize," Lucas slurred.

"No! You can wait until tomorrow," Jacqueline whispered.

"I cannot. I must court Lady Selina. The viper who shall become my bride."

Duncan growled and swirled Lucas around, landing a punch on the side of his cheek. In his drunken state, he missed Lucas's eye by a longshot. "You promised."

Lucas nodded, swaying on his feet. "That I did."

Jacqueline rushed over and knocked on Evelyn's room, asking Worthington to help Lucas and Duncan to their rooms before they caused any more damage. Since Abigail and Selina never opened their doors, she only hoped they slept through the entire debacle. Which was hoping for a miracle. She continued to her bedroom, where she pressed her hand against the closed door. She wanted to enter, but needed to clean up the mess from her cousins. With a sigh, she found a servant and helped them pick up the sharp fragments. In the meantime, Worthington settled Lucas and Duncan and joined Evelyn back in bed.

 Once she realized the house had returned to sleep, Jacqueline blew out the candles lighting the hallway and slipped back inside her bedroom. Only to find it empty. She leaned against the door, staring at the rumpled bed where she'd left a gentleman she greatly desired. She'd hoped he would have remained, but understood the reason for making his escape back to his own bedchamber. He made a wise decision in leaving when he had.

Jacqueline played with fire, carrying on an affair with the gentleman in her uncle's home. But they had fallen into this routine whenever he paid a visit. Which, to Jacqueline's delight, had been quite frequent these past few months. She knew her time to secure a groom grew near. And the lord who shared her bed wouldn't find any kind of acceptance from her uncle. He was a penniless peer and couldn't keep a bride in comfort, for his estate and lands were in disrepair.

It was a promising sign Jacqueline didn't involve her heart in their affair. She kept it securely closed from any tender affections. She might have gifted him with her body, but her heart would remain hers for all of eternity. Jacqueline suffered no lovesickness like her sisters and cousins. She chalked it up to their family's affliction of madness. Luckily, she was spared from any lovestruck curses.

She ran her fingers over her lips and remembered how he'd devoured them upon his arrival to her bedchamber. She smiled at the memories of their lovemaking.

Then she gasped. Jacqueline now understood the meaning behind Duncan's questions. Did he know? She hoped he was too drunk to remember. They would need to be more careful in the future in case Duncan questioned his suspicions. Duncan would confront her if so. If he didn't within the next couple of days, then they could resume their affair before her lover left again.

A wanton smile spread across her face as she thought about all the ways they could enjoy themselves.

Chapter Sixteen

Duncan realized what he risked by sneaking down the hallway to Selina's bedchamber. But he needed to see her.

He'd tried to reach her through the secret passageway, but found it locked from the outside. If his uncle thought a simple lock would stop him from his pursuit of Selina, he was sorely mistaken. He eased her door open and slipped inside. He wasn't as drunk as Lucas was. His cousin had drunk more than half the bottle. Duncan had just watched him, wanting to still have his wits about him so he could pay Selina a visit. A visit spent with many hours of loving her.

Selina never stirred, and he realized she slept deeply. He should let her rest, but he was too selfish to do so. He found a chair and tipped it under the doorknob to prevent anyone from walking in on them. Then he stripped his clothes and slid under the covers, pulling her into his arms. She mumbled, but kept on sleeping. Selina snuggled into him, and he realized he would have the pleasure of waking her up with his kisses. His caresses would awaken her from her deep sleep, and the desire he couldn't fulfill this afternoon would take hold.

He rolled her over and peeled her nightgown off her body. While most innocent maidens wore prim and proper garments, his lovely Selina wore scandalous gowns a mistress would wear. He wondered how she could purchase such nightwear. Duncan, however, was more than grateful for the sensuous garments. They cried sin, and Duncan was more than willing to do the garment justice. Perhaps another night he would enjoy it and let her keep it on while he brought them both to heights of pleasure.

Tonight, he only wanted to gaze upon her lush curves and savor the silkiness of her skin with his kisses.

He laid on his side, his fingers lightly caressing her. His thumb brushed across her nipple, and he watched it harden from his simple touch. A soft moan whispered across Selina's lips. He bent his head, drawing the bud between his lips, and suckled it gently. His tongue flicked back and forth, savoring the sweetness. He cupped her breast. The full weight nestled in his grip, and he squeezed it tenderly and sucked her nipple harder. Selina arched her chest closer and whimpered. Duncan opened his eyes, looking up to see her lids remained closed, her body answering its needs all on its own.

His mouth continued its assault, loving her breasts while his hand continued the path along the length of her body. Lightly touching. Teasing. Her body reacted to his touch, shifting to where she thought he might caress her next. Duncan didn't disappoint her. No point on her body went neglected. He brushed across her curls, and a sensual moan echoed around the room. When his fingers glided into her wetness, he released his own moan of pleasure. Christ, she was soaked. He pulled his hand away, noticing the glistening dew, and his cock grew harder, demanding its release.

Selina whimpered at the absence of his touch, and he returned his hand, stroking her body to a feverish height, surely to awaken her. Still, she slept and never spoke his name. Before he continued, he wanted her awake and calling his name in the throes of passion. His caresses stopped, and he waited.

"Selina, love," Duncan whispered.

"Mmm."

"Open your eyes."

Selina hovered on the edge of consciousness, refusing to wake from the dream where Duncan worshipped her body. Even though he teased her with his soft touch, he made her ache for him to claim her as his. Still, his kisses kept Selina from opening her eyes. She arched her body, taking pleasure at how he sucked, nipped, and licked her breasts. If only it were real. She needed Duncan to possess her soul again. The dream was bittersweet, but achingly so.

His whisper plea begged her to open her eyes. She could never deny him, even if she wanted to. No, Duncan Forrester controlled her heart and soul and would do so forever. She wondered if she followed his demand, would her dream fade away or become a reality? Selina realized it was already fading away when his touch halted. She wanted to cry from the loss. Her eyes fluttered open, waiting for the anguish to become a reality.

However, she found Duncan staring intently at her with a passion her body craved for him to fulfill. It hadn't been a dream, after all. All along, her body responded to having its need satisfied by the man of her dreams. He had stroked her every sense, awakening her with his soft touches and gentle kisses. Once her gaze met his, he slid his fingers inside her. At her gasp, his lips claimed her, drawing out her need with each stroke of his tongue against hers. With each kiss he strung from her lips, his fingers demanded her capitulation with its relentless pursuit of her release.

"Surrender yourself and come fully awake, Duchess. I am here for you," Duncan whispered as his fingers plunged inside her, his thumb stroking across her clit. His spoken declaration heightened her need to unravel in his embrace. Selina answered his request by clinging to him and pulling his head down to scream her pleasure into his kiss.

Selina unraveled under his touch and fell apart in his embrace. Her body, once strung tightly with need, softened underneath him. Her kisses turned slower and softer. Her hands started their own travel over his body. Duncan responded to her touch. His body had never received a touch so gentle before. He savored her attention, aching for it to never stop.

Selina's release only made Duncan hunger for more. He needed to savor her sweetness this night. He craved the succulent delicacy. While his touch had started out gentle, his need ate away at him for release. He wouldn't find satisfaction until Selina was his in every manner this evening. His hunger grew, needing to be fulfilled. His caress turned more passionate, his kisses more demanding. Selina responded in kind, answering his need with her own.

She knew the exact moment when Duncan's mood shifted. His hunger became more demanding with each bold stroke. While his lips devoured her body with kiss after kiss, they each struck their own spark to the flames of their desire. His need to possess her rang clear when his tongue pressed against her wetness. Her own body opened to his possession by wrapping herself around him. She lost control with each flick of his tongue. Each stroke of his finger. Each time he drank from her wetness he moaned his pleasure. His scandalous words whispered for her to unleash her passion on his lips.

Selina needed to touch him. Any part of him while he devoured her. Her fingers clutched his hair, pulling his head closer to her core. She rotated her hips to give him better access to pleasuring her. Her body rocked to each thrust of his tongue. She gave into Duncan's immense hold of her senses. Selina lost herself to the insanity and succumbed to the madness of his loving.

Nothing had ever tasted as sweet as Selina on his tongue. He breathed in her very essence as he claimed her. With each caress, she fed him with her need. Until his last dying breath, he would never find satisfaction and would hunger for another taste of her. Her fingers gripped his head and guided him to satisfy her need, her body moving in time with him. His fingers dug into her buttocks as he devoured her. Each time she hit her climax, her pleasure vibrated on his tongue. Still, it wasn't enough for him. It would never be enough. He drank from her until his body demanded its release.

He rose above her and slid inside her with one deep thrust. Each thrust went deeper and harder than the one before, answering his body's demands. She belonged with him and no other. His desperation clung to their lovemaking. He could not lose her.

Once again, Duncan's lovemaking shifted to one Selina herself felt. Each stroke declared how fragile their connection held itself together and how close they were to losing it. Selina wrapped herself closer to Duncan, matching his desperate need with her own. She would soon lose him and give herself to another. But in her selfishness, she kept allowing him to make love to her. It only made her more desperate to reach the pleasure they both needed to ease the ache consuming them.

Selina pressed her hips into Duncan's and swiveled them. She gasped at how the intimate contact pressed him deeper inside and built her need more fiercely. She raked her fingernails down his back when his strokes grew faster.

Selina struck her claws on him, causing Duncan to lose control. Her nipples scraped across his chest, and her hips made demands he so willingly complied with. Selina had wrapped herself around him and clung like a vine, making him believe in their love. Only an illusion to fool him in this heartbreaking beat of time.

"Selina, I …"

Selina pressed her finger against his lips. "Shh. Only love me during this precious time we stole. No more right now. My heart cannot handle it. Only love me."

Duncan nodded, not trusting himself to speak. The sadness in her voice kept him from declaring his love. He answered the need in her by fulfilling her request. He loved her. His body declared the love he held for her by sending them into eternal bliss.

Selina floated from Duncan's lovemaking. He clasped her in his embrace and kept placing kisses on her head while his hands softly caressed her body, bringing her down from a high she had never felt before. He never spoke a word, only holding and loving her throughout the night. She only closed her eyes again when he dressed and stole from her bedroom in the early morning before dawn. His lovemaking throughout the night was gentle and unforgettable. Whenever she tried to speak, he only repeated her actions, holding a finger to her lips and shaking his head. When he left without a kiss, it was then Selina understood the depth of her selfish actions and the heartache it would leave in its destruction.

The sadness in his eyes reflected her own.

Chapter Seventeen

Selina woke the next morning in a foggy haze to a flurry of activity in her bedchamber. She sat up quickly, drawing the quilt to her chest. Luckily, she'd had the good sense to draw on her nightgown and a robe after Duncan left. If not, she would have much to explain for lying in a rumpled bed without wearing a stitch of clothing. She swiped the sleep in her eyes, thinking what she witnessed was an illusion.

Instead of waking to the wonderful dream of Duncan making love to her, she now awoke to a nightmare starring the Holbrooke sisters and Abigail Cason, with Gemma trailing behind them wearing a smirk.

Gemma's arrival thrilled Selina. However, she remained on guard with the other ladies' visit. They had made their stand clear over the last two weeks, and she wondered about the sudden change. Charlie directed the servants where to sit the hot chocolate and pastries. Each of the ladies gathered their drink and food and settled into a seat. Gemma sat next to Selina on the bed and gathered her into a hug. Selina hadn't realized how much she needed that until now.

"You came," said Selina.

Gemma laughed. "Of course. I told you I would not miss your wedding."

Silence descended on the group at her declaration. There wasn't a single soul in the bedroom who wanted this marriage to occur. Selina least of all.

Selina attempted a smile. "I am glad you are here."

Gemma nodded, then poured two cups of hot chocolate and filled a plate full of breakfast edibles. A servant helped Gemma carry the items over to the bed, and she settled against the headboard. Selina accepted the cup and took a sip, glancing around to find every eye upon her filled with curiosity.

"Thank you, Polly. That will be all," said Jacqueline.

After the maid left, conversation erupted with excitement. Selina grew still, unsure how to react. They acted as if this were an everyday occurrence. It was for them, but they had never once invited Selina to take part in their early morning ritual. She didn't understand what had changed to make this morning any different.

After Duncan left her at dawn, she'd grown too exhausted for her early morning ride with Ramsay. She'd sent word of her apologies and informed her maid she would sleep longer. She'd fallen back into a deep sleep, but visions of Duncan kept hovering within her reach. Now she sat in unchartered territory, not knowing what to expect.

"So do spill. Was the honeymoon as scandalous as the courtship?" Charlie waggled her eyebrows.

Gemma's twinkling laughter filled the room. "Even more so."

"Details, cousin. We want to hear the details. Did he make you …" Charlie urged.

"Charlie! You are going to give Lady Selina the wrong impression," Jacqueline reprimanded.

Selina sat in shock at how easily they conversed of such private matters and even more so at Jacqueline's defense.

"In Charlie's defense, if she is to become one of us, she must become accustomed to how we behave." Evelyn bit into a scone.

Jacqueline shook her head. "Worthington has corrupted you."

Evelyn smiled cheekily. "Yes, he has, much to my delight."

Jacqueline threw her hands in the air. "Your marriages have made both of you wicked."

Gemma sighed. "A most proper marriage will hold that effect over a lady."

Charlie laughed. "There is nothing proper to any of our marriages."

Charlie, Evelyn, and Gemma all laughed at the truth of the statement, causing Jacqueline and Abigail to shake their heads in defeat. But the smiles on their faces spoke otherwise. They smiled at the other ladies fondly, happy for their successful marriages. The usual ping of envy washed over Selina at their friendship. She secretly wished to be a part of it.

Gemma set her cup on the nightstand and covered her hands over her stomach. "I have a bit of news to share with you."

"You and Ralston are expecting," Abigail guessed quietly.

Gemma nodded, and the bed shook when each lady crowded around Gemma for a hug. Selina hadn't realized tears slid along her cheeks at watching their excitement over Gemma's news. They took pleasure in each other's happiness, which only left Selina more depressed than ever. When they pulled away, they resumed their seats, talking excitedly about the baby news.

"Congratulations," Selina whispered, not wanting to draw attention to herself.

Gemma's smile dropped. "Why are you crying?"

"I am so happy for you."

"Oh, Selina, you poor dear. Has it been so awful of late?"

Selina attempted to smile in an effort to present her acceptance of her situation but failed. She shook her head, too choked to voice her displeasure. Especially in front of the other ladies.

Jacqueline answered for Selina. "I fear that is our fault. We did not take your request to heart, Gemma. Instead, we kept with our determination to make Selina feel as unwelcome as possible. As a result of us harboring our resentment of the situation, we failed to see how Selina was just as much of a victim."

Gemma shook her head in disappointment, rising from the bed. "How do I even express my displeasure at each of you? You each made me a promise and have failed to discover Selina's true character. Aunt Susanna wrote to me of Selina's attempt to rectify her past actions, but it appears while she has grown, each of you has sunken to a depth I am ashamed of."

Abigail rose and guided Gemma to sit again. "Do not upset yourself, 'tis not good for the babe. You stand correct in your shame." She turned to Selina. "Please forgive my actions. It was not until yesterday when Lucas lashed out at you and Duncan defended your cause that I realized you are more of a victim than any of us. You had no choice in the arrangement your father decided for your future. You were only groomed to accept it as your fate. I hope you will accept my apology and offer of friendship."

Selina wiped the tears off her cheek. "I apologize for my unkindness in the past to everyone. At the end of the season, I realized how my past actions caused a rift where a pleasant relationship would never happen. I fear jealousy and loneliness prompted my poor behavior, and it has only come to my attention of late what a sincere friendship really is. I understand if none of you will ever consider me a friend, but I can only hope we can get along in the foreseeable future."

"What Abigail attempted to relate is that we are all at fault, and we wish to apologize for our own mistreatment. The reason for our invasion is to offer you our friendship in the days to come." Jacqueline smiled, and everyone nodded in agreement.

"Really?" asked Selina, doubting she heard correctly.

Abigail smiled. "Really."

A smile lit up Selina's face. "I do not know what to say."

Evelyn laughed. "You do not need to say a word. You only must agree to join us for morning hot chocolate and scones whenever Uncle Theo does not demand our attendance at the breakfast table."

Selina nodded. "Then you have my agreement."

Charlie rubbed her hands together. "Excellent. Now we can move on to more important matters."

"Charlie!" Evelyn and Jacqueline spoke at once.

"What? There is a wedding but a week away. If we do not intervene, then who knows what Uncle Theo has planned."

"Charlie has a point. When I questioned him before I wed, he told me not to interfere, that Selina and Lucas would wed," said Gemma.

"But did he say they would wed each other?" asked Charlie.

Gemma shook her head. "He did not specify."

"And Duncan is under the impression Uncle Theo invited him to town for a different result," interjected Evelyn.

"For Duncan and Selina to make a match?" asked Abigail.

Jacqueline started laughing uncontrollably. "Exactly. Why, that sneaky devil and his matchmaking madness."

Selina's brows drew together. "I do not understand."

"Oh, my dear friend, I fear you are the latest to fall victim in Uncle Theo's trap. Our uncle thinks of himself as a matchmaker of sorts, and Aunt Susanna is his co-conspirator," Gemma explained.

"I still do not understand. Why does he want to make a match for me, when I am already set to marry his son?" Realization dawned on Selina, and she paled while answering her own question. "Because he does not find me suitable enough to become Lucas's wife."

"No, no, no. 'Tis not the reason at all." Abigail rushed to sit next to Selina, pulling her hand to hold between hers.

Everyone stared in shock at Abigail comforting Selina. Yes, they had all made their apologies to the beauty, but Abigail soothing her surprised them. Abigail was the very reason Uncle Theo had tried to make a different match for Selina.

Selina's eyes widened at the friendly gesture. "What else could be the reason?"

"Colebourne feels guilty…" Abigail began.

"Abigail," Gemma growled.

Abigail sighed, shaking her head. "*Uncle Theo* has learned of my feelings regarding Lucas. He has decided we would make a perfect match, but the betrothal agreement has tied his hands. He believes if he found another gentleman for you to fall in love with, you will plead for your father to release you from the contract."

"Do you love Lucas?" Selina whispered.

Abigail nodded.

"Does Lucas love you?" Selina asked.

"Yes," the other ladies answered, but Abigail followed with, "No, I do not believe he does. He only sees me as a responsibility."

Selina regarded Abigail shrewdly. "I disagree. He never takes his eyes off you, and he obsesses over your every move."

Abigail blushed. "Your eyes deceive you."

Selina smiled wistfully. "No, they do not. What a mess. For years, I had been told of my destiny. Never questioning it, but only following the demands of my father. I was always secure in the knowledge that Lucas would become my husband. Even watching him always watch you, I knew he was mine. I thought no differently until ..." Selina trailed off.

"Until one Duncan Forrester broke down your walls and made you question everything you had ever been told," answered Charlie.

This time Selina was the one who wore a blush. "Yes. Is it more than obvious?"

"Only to those of us who have walked in your shoes of late," soothed Evelyn.

"I have no clue what to do. I fear Duncan only fools with me, even though his whispered words speak differently."

"I disagree. He would not risk your reputation if his heart were not engaged. You may risk your father's wrath, but Duncan risks the wrath of our uncle. Not to mention his bond with Lucas," Jaqueline explained. "And sneaking time alone with you only shows what he risks for loving you."

Selina's face flamed from embarrassment. What must these ladies think of her for betraying Lucas? "You must think me so wanton. I never intended for any of this to happen. Duncan swept me up in this passion, and I wanted but a brief moment of happiness before I started my life with Lucas. It was selfish of me to do so. I do not wish to take Lucas from you, Abigail. But I know of no other way. My father will not allow me to break the contract."

This time, Abigail asked the question. "Do you love Duncan?

Selina nodded.

Everyone in the room squealed, including Abigail.

Gemma clapped. "Excellent. Now we must do our own scheming. Upon my arrival, I overheard Uncle Theo conspiring with Aunt Susanna on the seating arrangement for future meals. He was very explicit in his orders. Duncan is never to have a seat next to you. You will sit next to Lucas and a gentleman of Uncle Theo's choosing. Between now and the wedding, you must convince Lucas how horrible his life would become if he married you."

"How? I already showed him how much of a shrew I am, and while he shows his disappointment in me, he hasn't tried to break the agreement himself."

Jacqueline took a sip of the lukewarm hot chocolate. "Only you can break the contract, Selina, and no one else."

Selina shook her head in denial. "No. The clause written in the contract states either party can break it if they found a more suitable match. But the match must bring forth the same, if not more of a substantial, gain. Which means Lucas cannot in the end. I mean no disrespect, Abigail."

Abigail smiled. "I understand my standings in society, and I know you mean no harm. 'Tis a matter of fact."

"The clause does not rule out Duncan," said Evelyn.

"Duncan nowhere matches what Lucas will bring into our marital union," Selina scoffed.

"But Duncan can …" Gemma tried to explain Duncan's worth.

Charlie interrupted with a conniving smile. "Yes, Duncan's worth is nowhere near Lucas's holdings. Selina must act the shrew again to make Lucas beg Uncle Theo to relent."

Gemma's stared at Charlie with curiosity about why she'd stopped her from explaining Duncan's worth when it was obvious Selina held no clue of his fortune. She wanted to inform Selina how Duncan could offer her more security than Lucas ever could, but Charlie had her reasons for withholding the truth. She would trust her cousin because she had never failed them before.

Evelyn held up a hand. "Hold on. I must ask. Are your reasons for not confessing to your father about Duncan because of his worth?"

"No. I only know of my father's refusal if I seek to break the betrothal and what his answer will be. If my father believed in love, then I would beg for release now. But my father is cynical and will only scoff at my love for Duncan. I love Duncan too fiercely to have it deemed an unnecessary emotion not belonging in a marital union." Selina's answer seemed to have found approval among the other ladies. "So you see, no matter what course I take, it is hopeless."

Gemma shook her head. "I disagree. The one thing I learned from my own, shall we say, courtship with Ralston was, in the end, Uncle Theo wanted us to take the risk and declare our love for one another. He only does this matchmaking business to see us settled. And you, Selina, have endeared yourself to him, and he only wishes the same for you too. I have changed my mind on how you should approach your time with Lucas. My best advice is for you to be yourself with Lucas in these coming days."

"But will that not convince him he can tolerate me as a wife?"

"No, it will make him analyze his feelings for Abigail more closely," Gemma replied.

Selina bit her lip. "I am not sure."

"Just try it, and we shall see what we can accomplish by convincing Lucas or Duncan into declaring their true intentions. That is what Uncle Theo wants. But beware of his tricks. Our uncle is a devious matchmaker," Evelyn encouraged.

Charlie laughed. "Do not forget Aunt Susanna too."

"And Ramsay?" asked Selina.

Jacqueline smiled. "No. He only shakes his head at their shenanigans. However, you have charmed him."

Before Selina could voice any objections to their suggestions, Lady Forrester bustled into the bedroom with Selina's maid following behind her. "Oh, how lovely of you girls to include Selina in your morning ritual. But I am afraid it must end. Selina needs to prepare for an afternoon visiting the tenants with Lucas."

Lady Forrester hustled the girls from the room. But Gemma stopped before Selina, drawing her into a hug. She whispered in Selina's ear, "Be yourself, and all will work out in the end."

Selina nodded, remembering the Duke of Colebourne had spoken words of a similar nature not so long ago. She remained quiet while Lady Forrester helped her prepare for the afternoon visits, listening with only half an ear. Her thoughts replayed the visit with the Holbrooke cousins and Abigail Cason. It was a visit she had waited a lifetime for, and it was everything she'd expected and more.

A tremendous weight of her past ill behavior lifted. Now a lighthearted joy of forming new friendships that would last a lifetime filled her soul. She should feel dread for the impending doom of her upcoming nuptials, but instead, hope bloomed in her heart. Perhaps with the help of her new friends, Selina and Duncan could declare their love for one another and live happily ever after.

Chapter Eighteen

Duncan hurried along the hallway, hoping to catch Selina and his father for their morning ride. He had overslept after spending many wonderful hours in her arms. He still hadn't figured out how he would invite himself along without his uncle discovering his deception, but he needed to try. Duncan paused when he heard the silly laughter of his cousins. He couldn't tell which bedroom they met in for their breakfast this morning. Only that they enjoyed each other's company, excluding Selina. He wanted to scold them for their cruel behavior, but he couldn't waste a second more.

He continued to the stables and requested his horse. While waiting, Duncan noticed his father's horse no longer sat in its stall. He'd missed them. Which was for the best. Now he could ride out and happen upon them by accident. Then no witness could report back to his uncle.

Duncan took off, squiring the countryside for any sign of them. He searched the village and neighboring estates, but he couldn't find them anywhere. On his return from Sinclair's land, he stopped at a nearby creek to cool down his horse and came upon his father fishing all by himself.

His father looked up at his arrival and shook his head. The disappointment in his father's gaze let Duncan know he was in for a lecture.

Duncan nodded toward the creek. "Catch anything yet?"

His father shook his head. "Nay. But from your desperation, neither have you."

Duncan scowled. "I am not desperate. However, where is your lovely riding companion?"

Ramsay shrugged. "Probably still in bed. You know how those pampered lasses are."

"Selina is not pampered, as you are well aware."

"Nay, she is. Sent word she wanted to lie in today."

Duncan advanced on his father. "Perhaps she is tired. I heard she retired early with a headache."

Ramsay arched a brow. "How do ye know about her ailment?"

"I heard her maid telling another servant when I returned from the stables last night."

Ramsay laughed. "Yes. I heard all about the punishment Colebourne handed to you and Lucas. I also notice how ye are disobeying your uncle."

Duncan spread his hands out. "How am I disobeying? I am out for a morning ride in which I ran into my father and stopped for a *friendly* conversation."

"You do not fool me, boy. Both of us know the reason behind your morning ride. I warned you. Now Colebourne has warned you. Do not take these warnings lightly. If not for your sake, then do it for the lass. She has much more to lose then ye."

"I cannot."

"You must. What happens when Lucas discovers you fool with his intended? He will not take it well. Not to mention Norbury can ruin you and all you hold dear. Is she worth it?"

"Aye."

His answer hung heavy between them. He spoke it firmly, with no hesitation. There was no other course for him. Selina was his destination. Their relationship went past a point of no return. They would hurt many with their union, and scandal would always follow in its wake. But he refused to deny their connection.

His father nodded in defeat. He had tried to warn Duncan away, but it was useless advice he wouldn't listen to. Duncan settled against a rock, watching his father throw his pole in and out of the pond. Neither of them spoke about Selina again. Soon, Duncan's late night crept upon him, and he dozed off. His father woke him up when the sun had moved high above them.

"It is time to ride back, lad. Your mother will wonder where I got off to."

Duncan staggered to his feet, still drowsy. He climbed onto his horse and looked over at his father. "I know I disappoint you. But I love her and cannot let her go."

Ramsay sighed. "You do not disappoint me. I only worry about the outcome of your affair if you do not win the lass. I see the love you hold for her. 'Tis the same I hold for your mother. Also, I care for the lass, and she does not deserve to live a heartbroken life. She has suffered enough, and there are too many obstacles standing in the way. Ones I doubt will fall in your favor."

Duncan smiled with confidence. "You underestimate me, Father. First and foremost, I am a Scotsman, and I always get what I want. If not, I will resort to the Scots' custom and steal what is mine."

Ramsay laughed. "Long live the Scots."

Duncan let out a battle cry. "Let's race, you ol' codger."

"Who ye calling old?" Ramsay yelled, racing his horse ahead of his son.

Duncan laughed, urging his horse on. Still, his father's horse was faster, and he never caught up with him. The fast ride was refreshing. It allowed all of his troubles to fade away with each stretch of land he passed. Once he reached the stables, his father goaded him about how slow he rode.

Duncan only smiled. After all, he was the one who kissed and loved the girl. The only outcome was for him to make her his bride. Everything else was inconsequential.

~~~~~

Selina rested on a settee between Lady Forrester and Abigail in the drawing room. The ladies had retired for tea while the gentleman drank their brandy and smoked their cigars. Colebourne favored the vile habit, much to Selina's dislike. Her father only ever smoked them in Colebourne's company. When Selina inquired why he did, he told her one must partake in such habits to please others. It never made much sense to her. At least Lucas didn't find the habit pleasing. During their time together, he never smelled of smoke. Neither had Duncan whenever they kissed.

Duncan and his kisses. She never thought she would miss those as she had these past few days. He'd avoided her at all costs, confusing her with his true intentions. With her wedding day drawing nearer, had he changed his mind? Was she only someone to fool with? Did he plot with Lucas to involve her in a scandal so Lucas could call off the wedding?

Doubts plagued her thoughts constantly. Any time she voiced them, her new friends would silence them with reassurances, reminding her of Colebourne's plans to keep them apart. If only Duncan would stare her way, then the power of his gaze would reassure her, but he made himself scarce, never stealing time alone with her.

Lady Forrester talked to Lady Worthington in the chair next to her. Guests for the wedding had arrived throughout the day. They were discussing those dreaded flower arrangements again. Thankfully, Lady Forrester didn't include Selina in the conversation. Abigail talked gaily with Noel and Eden Worthington, describing the local village and how she would show them around on the morrow. After a while, the Worthington sisters rose and moved to sit next to Gemma. Selina kept watching the door, hoping the gentlemen would join them soon.

"Staring at the door will not make him magically appear," Abigail teased.

Selina tried to smile. "One could only hope he will."

"Even if he does, he will keep his distance," Abigail whispered, not wanting to draw Lady Forrester's attention.

Selina nodded. She knew he would avoid her, no matter how much her heart wished differently. "I miss him."

"Duncan returns your sentiment."

Selina scoffed. "I beg to differ. He has avoided me since he came to my…" She felt her face warm from what she'd almost confessed.

Abigail tilted her head. "Since when?"

Selina tried to recover. "Since our visit in the parlor, before Lucas and you interrupted us."

"Interrupted you from what, exactly?"

Selina's face flamed. She only dug herself in deeper. "What I am trying to explain is that we have not spoken for days."

Abigail's eyes widened at Selina's nervousness. It never came to her mind that Selina and Duncan's relationship had advanced to an intimate nature. She assumed they'd shared a few kisses, but nothing more. If this were the truth, then instead of keeping them separated to force Duncan to make his claim toward Selina, they needed to place them in each other's company.

Abigail's gaze swung around the room, trying to locate Charlie. Charlie would know how to proceed. She was the most devious of them and held a close relationship with Duncan. She found Charlie leaning against the terrace doors all by herself, staring out into the night. Charlie hated being stuck indoors, always craving the freedom she found outside.

Abigail patted Selina's hand. "I am sure you two will speak soon." Abigail rose abruptly and left Selina alone with Lady Forrester.

"Who will you speak with soon?" asked Lady Forrester.

Selina watched Abigail rush across the room and pull Charlie onto the terrace. She wondered what was so important for her to leave. Selina slowly turned her head toward Lady Forrester, but her gaze stayed firmly on Charlie and Abigail. They were outside the terrace doors, and Abigail whispered feverishly while glancing back at Selina. Charlie started shaking with laughter, and Abigail reprimanded her. Selina knew she was the topic of their discussion, and her insecurities rose to the surface again. She lost sight of them when they stepped farther into the shadows. Selina shifted, trying to catch them in her viewpoint.

Lady Forrester voiced her question again, and in her distraction, Selina blurted out the name of the gentleman on her mind. "Duncan."

Selina gasped, her gaze finally connecting with Lady Forrester's. She covered her hand over her mouth. "I meant Lucas. I wanted to ask him what our plans were for tomorrow."

Lady Forrester smiled wickedly. "Of course, dear. Who else but your intended would you wish to see?"

"Yes. Yes, of course. Lucas—I mean ... Lord Gray promised a walk around the garden this evening."

"You may call him Lucas. After all, we are all family, are we not?"

"Yes, we shall be soon." Selina's voice resounded with sadness. Every reminder of her impending marriage made her grow more despondent and desperate for her destiny to change.

Lady Forrester wanted to comfort the girl with reassurances. But Selina's life still hung in the balance and would remain so, unless all the parties involved in this love triangle confessed to their feelings. Duty and honor were strange bedfellows and prompted one to set aside their true desires for what others expected of them or for what they thought they should do. Her own anxiety grew the longer her son refused to declare his intentions. When Colebourne suggested a match between the two, she had been skeptical at first, until she saw the spark between Duncan and Selina and realized they were soul mates. Her son, while charming, was also exasperating. A trait he'd inherited from his father.

Lady Forrester decided she couldn't remain patient any longer. After all, this was her son's happiness on the line. She decided to give her own nudge in this madness. "Ramsay and I would be proud to call you our daughter."

Selina's eyes widened, and she glanced around the drawing room to see if anyone had overheard Lady Forrester. "Pardon?"

"Selina, dear. I must be frank with you because we have little time."

Selina kept looking around. "I do not think this is an appropriate conversation. Especially in the company of others."

Lady Forrester waved her hand. "Pshh. There is not a single lady in this room who would find fault with you for following your heart. I know my nieces are aware of your feelings for my son, or else they would not have finally formed friendships with you. As for the Worthington ladies, they are family and can see the dynamics between you and Duncan. Everyone can see, and we approve. Well, everyone but your fiancé. He is as clueless toward you as he is to the love Abigail holds for him. But that is another matter Colebourne has plans for."

"Plans? As in matchmaking?"

Lady Forrester laughed. "Ahh, I see the girls have let you in on our family's shenanigans. I am sure they have declared it madness." She shrugged. "Perhaps it is, but it helped to secure their happiness, as it will yours."

"I do not see how. I am set to wed Lucas. You are planning the wedding."

"True. But if you can convince Lucas to break the betrothal, then you will have solved your problem."

Selina shook her head. "I have tried. But everything I do only makes him seek my company out more. Even today, I kept switching up my behavior. I was nice one minute, then a shrew the next. I confused myself. Still, he kept continuing on with an engaging conversation throughout dinner and asked me to join him for a stroll around the gardens after they finish drinking their brandy."

"I fear Colebourne has pressed his issue for Lucas to pay you attention or he will force the wedding to happen sooner. I'm betraying Colebourne's confidence by informing you of his plans. But my first responsibility is to my son and his happiness. And you are his happiness. Now we only need to convince Lucas to abandon you and for Duncan to sweep in and steal you away."

Selina bit her lip. "How?"

Lady Forrester smiled mischievously. "Why, with the proven strategy of all time, my dear."

"And that is?"

"Good old-fashioned jealousy, of course."

Selina was still confused. "Why would I want to make Lucas jealous?"

"Not Lucas, but Duncan. You must persuade Lucas to kiss you on your walk. It will solve two birds with one stone. One, Lucas will think you are a forward miss and question your character as his duchess. The other will show Duncan what he will have to watch if your union to Lucas comes to be and prompt him to declare his love and stop your wedding."

Selina winced. "It is most dishonest. And I cannot find myself even tempted to kiss Lucas. The very thought unsettles my nerves."

Lady Forrester narrowed her gaze. "Yes, that was probably not the best suggestion. How about you convince Lucas to draw you into an embrace of comfort? Can you manage that? I am sure if my son saw Lucas's hands upon you, it will set a rise to his Scottish temper."

Selina thought over Lady Forrester's suggestion. She didn't wish to anger Duncan, but she felt more desperate than ever. She also didn't wish to deceive anyone, either. Her friendship with Lucas's cousins was too new to ask if she should take Lady Forrester's advice. What should she do?

It no longer mattered anyway because the door opened and the gentleman arrived, putting a stop to their conversation. Selina waited for Duncan to stroll through for a glance at him. When he walked in with Lucas by his side, laughing over something, her heart dropped. Every guilty thought consumed her, making her feel suffocated with the actions she'd taken since her arrival. She decided, after her walk with Lucas, she would confront her father and confess to her betrayal.

Her father would demand her silence and still force her to wed Lucas. She already knew the outcome of the conversation. But she would speak the truth. When she finished with her father, she would throw herself at the mercy of the Duke of Colebourne and beg him to release her from the contract. Over the years, she had squired away a small amount of money in case her father disowned her.

Because he would do so once she confessed her sins.

Chapter Nineteen

Duncan scowled from his position of leaning against the fireplace mantle. He watched his cousin charm the woman Duncan loved. Her face lit from the pleasure of his attention. Did Selina fall for Lucas's sudden change of infatuation? It would appear so with the smile she gifted him. It was full of lighthearted joy, and her eyes glowed with glee. He itched with jealousy. She'd shared the same expression with him recently. He foolishly thought she only gifted him the look since he had never seen her display it toward another. It was only an illusion.

Every time he sought Selina out, someone stepped in his path, blocking any attempt to gain her attention. At first, he believed himself unlucky, but then he grew suspicious when he noticed the ladies of his family had befriended Selina. While one of them occupied her time, the others kept him distracted. He sensed a conspiracy against him. Even his own mother and father warned him away from her.

Then whenever he caught his uncle's eye, he would quirk his brow and smirk at him, taunting Duncan to disobey him. Uncle Theo even stationed a servant in the passageway. After he disengaged the lock in his bedroom, he found a servant patrolling the dark space. Duncan knew the servant had informed his uncle of his own prowling because the following morning he received a note of warning from his uncle. If Duncan attempted to seek out Selina, he would follow through with his threat.

His gaze narrowed as he took in the scene before him. Lucas and Selina acted the perfect couple, making their way around the drawing room as if they were the hosts. When they stopped at the small group with Charlie, Evelyn, and their husbands, the ladies giggled over a remark Sinclair made.

The wiggling doubt of something not quite right flared again. Of all his family members, Charlie disliked Selina the most. Now she acted as if they were bosom friends. Charlie even laid her hand on Selina's arm in an affectionate gesture.

Somehow, without his knowledge, his footsteps drew him closer to the small group. He kept his distance, but he overheard Selina excusing herself to grab her shawl for their walk in the garden. The moment he'd been waiting for had finally arrived. However, he must be careful no one noticed him leaving.

Instead of following her out of the door, he slipped out onto the terrace. If anyone watched his progress, they would think he strolled toward the gardens. However, he stole around the corner and made his way through the servants' entrance. Once there, he climbed the stairs that led to the wing where their bedrooms were located.

He caught the sight of Selina's skirts as she hurried into her bedchamber. He glanced around to make sure no one followed him and hurried toward her. Duncan pulled the door closed and leaned against it, drinking in Selina's backside as she dug in her wardrobe. A most becoming sight. His body responded, begging to touch her. He wondered how she would respond if he were to lift her skirts and take her from behind. Duncan chuckled. He would probably gain a slap for his intentions if he were to proceed with them. His laughter caught her attention.

Selina gasped when she heard someone behind her. She rose slowly and found Duncan leaning against the door with a devilish glint in his eyes. She gulped, well aware of what his gaze meant. It was purely predatory. She clutched her shawl in front of her for protection. Which was foolish because no flimsy garment would keep Duncan from seducing her. And in truth, she needed no protection from what she desired, too. However, she didn't move any closer to him.

"Duncan, you should not be in my bedchamber."

Duncan pushed off from the door. "Why not? You did not deny my attention a few nights ago in this very room."

"'Tis most improper when others can notice. I do not wish to cause a scandal," Selina stammered.

Duncan nodded. "Ah, so the virtue of Selina Pemberton matters now that her bridegroom pays her an ounce of attention," Duncan snarled.

Selina shook her head. "No, you misunderstand."

Duncan took a step forward again. "No, I do not believe I do. Tell me, my love, have you enjoyed your time with Lucas these last few days playing husband and wife?"

Selina took a step back, only for the wardrobe to stop her retreat. She pressed her back up against it, realizing Duncan had trapped her. "Yes. My time spent with Lucas has been pleasant."

Duncan stepped closer. "You make quite a striking couple."

Selina's lips trembled. "Thank you."

Duncan stared at Selina, noting the vulnerability pouring from her responses. Her tongue snuck out to wet her trembling lips. Duncan groaned at the tempting sight of her succulent lips that begged for a kiss. How he wished to stroke his tongue across them and taste a sample of her sweetness. But he needed answers to ease the doubts consuming his thoughts.

He slid a few tendrils of hair that escaped her coiffure behind her ears. His fingers lingered over the soft strands. "Do you not question why Lucas pays you attention?"

"Because I need to learn the duties required of me for when I become his wife. Lucas has offered to teach them to me."

His fingers trailed along her neck, stopping at the thudding of her pulse. "So you still insist on following through with this debacle?"

Selina willed herself to move, but Duncan's powerful focus kept her in place. "Why would I not? It is the very reason I am at Colebourne Manor. Your mother has made the arrangements for the ceremony in two days. The guests have arrived, the kitchen prepares the cake, and the gardener has cut the flowers. My fiancé finally dances to my every whim. What other reason would I have not to marry Lucas Gray?"

Selina's speech grew more furious as she listed off every reason she planned to wed Lucas. She was baiting Duncan, hoping for any kind of reaction to give her a reason to halt the wedding. For days, she had waited for any sign from him to stop this madness, but he'd stayed away from her, avoiding her at all costs. She thought over how she'd decided earlier to confess to her father and Colebourne, and now realized it was only a silly girl's infatuation. A rakish scoundrel seduced her with his Scottish brogue. He sprinkled enough charm to leave her in doubt about her actions. Even now he toyed with her emotions, pretending to stake a claim on her.

Duncan pressed himself closer against Selina so she could feel the very evidence of why she shouldn't marry his cousin. A cruel bark of laughter escaped from his lips. "You believe Lucas dances to your whims.

Oh, *Duchess,* you are priceless. Lucas only follows his father's orders. Believe me when I say he loathes spending time in your company."

Selina glared at Duncan. "You lie."

Duncan's smile turned hard. "Do I?"

Selina pressed against his chest, trying to push him away. "Yes. He seeks my company every time I turn around. Even now, he waits for me to take a stroll through the gardens."

Duncan was immovable. "An act, my dear. All an act." His thumb brushed back and forth across her lower lip. "Tell me, have you let him kiss these sweet lips yet?" He lowered his head, his mouth but a breath away from hers. "Has he savored your sweetness as I have?"

Selina grew conflicted. Her body cried out from Duncan's nearness. However, his taunting words infuriated her. She'd come to terms with how she could share a friendly marriage with Lucas. Now Duncan threw down his taunts, making her believe her time spent with Lucas was a farce. Anger, need, heartache, desire, loneliness, and an ever-consuming passion swirled inside of her, each emotion seeking its release.

"I bet he has not even tried. Which only goes to prove he is not attracted to you. You hold no temptation for him." Duncan brushed his lips softly against hers, murmuring, "But do not fret, love, for you are the temptation of every sinful fantasy I have."

A resounding slap sent Duncan reeling back. His face stung from Selina's reaction. Then he realized how his foolish words had affected her. In his attempt to prove Lucas's attention was false, his cruel words had speared her heart instead. Tears clung to her eyelashes, but in her fury, she refused to allow them to drop. Her gazed narrowed on him, and her lips took on a pinched expression. It was then he knew she kept her anger barely controlled. Her hands curled into fists at her side, and she lifted her chin with pride before she attacked him. An attack he deserved with every controlled word she spoke.

Selina shook with rage and blinked her tears away. She wouldn't show him any side of her vulnerability. "You have the audacity to make a mockery of how Lucas and I behave together, when all along you have toyed with my emotions, making me believe something stronger forged our connection, when all along they were only a *scoundrel's sinful fantasies.* Well, Lord Forrester, I am afraid you will have to ease your ache with the village harlot because I am no longer at your mercy."

Before Duncan could react, Charlie burst into the room. "Selina, Lucas awaits your return. I told him I would check …" Charlie stopped in mid-sentence once she saw Duncan reaching for Selina and felt the tension in the room. "Selina? Duncan?"

Selina bent over to retrieve the shawl she had dropped when Duncan had pressed himself intimately against her. She took one last glance at Duncan and hurried away, not even offering Charlie an explanation for her delay.

Duncan tried to reach out and grab Selina before she left, but Charlie blocked him. "Selina!" Duncan yelled after her.

"Duncan, let her go."

Duncan snarled. "Step out of my way or I will remove you myself."

Charlie stepped to the side, waiting to speak until Duncan stepped into the hallway. "In my opinion, you should not follow her. She seemed most upset with you. Why bother anyway? You have had your fun. Now let her marry Lucas and count yourself lucky you do not have to marry her yourself."

Duncan stopped and turned slowly at Charlie's bait. "Lucky?"

Charlie laughed. "Yes. It would appear from the set-down you received, the dragon is breathing her fire again. I knew she could not keep it contained for long. And to think she fooled us with her act of playing the victim of being misunderstood and how nobody loves her."

"You are the lucky one, cousin."

Charlie tilted her head. "How so?"

"That she gifted her friendship to you, allowing you to see what a wonderful soul she has. That she allowed you to sit in her presence without bowing at her feet as the duchess she is. That she spoke a kind word to you at all."

Duncan turned again to chase after Selina when Charlie spoke. "You are correct again, my friend."

Duncan sighed and turned back again, finally realizing he'd missed his chance to catch Selina. Charlie wouldn't let him leave until she had her say. "Am I?"

"We harshly misjudged Selina, and thankfully, through this messed-up affair, we have found friendship with her. But, Duncan, you must see what you require of her is beyond what she is capable of. The demands placed on her are unfair, but what you ask for her to sacrifice is utter madness."

Duncan ran his hands through his hair in frustration. "You think I do not know that myself?"

"Then why were you so cruel to her before I walked in?"

Duncan winced. "You heard?"

Charlie nodded. "Aye."

Duncan sat on the bed and laid back, throwing his arm over his eyes. "Because the very thought of Lucas kissing Selina kills me. It feels like someone keeps punching me in the gut the closer this wedding draws near. I reacted without thinking, as usual."

Charlie sat down on the bed next to him. "Why did you have to ruin her?"

Duncan lifted his arm. "You know of that too?" Charlie nodded. "How?"

"Selina let something slip while talking to Abigail. We figured out you two might have been intimate. And you have now confirmed it. Why?"

Duncan turned toward Charlie. "I could not resist her. She is the other half of my soul. I cannot explain the emotions she inspires in me. It is too overwhelming."

Charlie gave Duncan a smile full of pity. "No need to. I understand myself. 'Tis how I feel about Jasper. The family's lovesick madness has struck you in the heart. There is no hope for you."

Duncan jumped off the bed and pulled Charlie to her feet. "That is where you are wrong, lass. I may possess the trait of madness, but my luck will prevail. Shall we return to the drawing room? I must apologize to a certain lady, and time is slipping away to woo her into becoming my bride."

Charlie patted his hand. "I wish you the best of luck."

He needed all the luck everyone could give him and then some. His behavior had been atrocious, and he needed to humble himself at her feet. Jealousy was a bitter pill to swallow, but one he must if he had any hope of convincing Selina of his love.

He only hoped he wasn't too late.

~~~~~~

Selina stopped once she rounded the corner to gather herself. Her twisted emotions kept ricocheting around in her heart. But she knew what she must do. She had to fulfill her obligations by marrying Lucas. What choice did she have? Duncan had ruined her, and from what he'd just shared with her, she was only a temptation he amused himself with. Nothing more. What made matters worse was that Lucas's behavior of late was false too. But it was one she could deal with because it caused her no heartache, unlike Duncan's conduct.

Was she mad to even consider marrying into this family? What other options did she have? She wasn't brave enough to walk away from what her father had planned. To do so would be a lonelier life than she already endured. If she married Lucas, she could still see Duncan. She wouldn't betray her wedding vows, but seeing him over the years would help to ease her heartache. It would be her punishment for the scandalous memories she captured for herself. A temptation always out of her grasp.

It was fitting for all the destruction she had caused. She would own up to her mistakes with her head held high. Because there was no other alternative. She refused to keep it down in shame. No, because duchesses didn't behave in that manner. After all, she was destined to become one.

Selina heard Charlie and Duncan walking along the hallway, and she scurried down the stairs, rushing into the drawing room. She found Lucas talking to Abigail and interrupted them. She was most rude to her new friend, but she couldn't help it. Selina needed to escape, and Lucas was her only means. She would apologize to Abigail later. For now, she apologized to Lucas for the delay, and he swept her out the doors toward the garden.

Selina barely kept up with Lucas. His frown grew fiercer, and his stride quickened. The pebbles in the path dug into her feet as she ran to stay by his side. Her ankle twisted, and she fell, clutching at Lucas's suit coat.

When she yelped, he stopped abruptly, causing Selina to slam into him. He grabbed a hold of her before she fell to the ground.

"Please forgive me, Lady Selina. I forgot I was in the company of another for a moment."

Selina gasped at the affront. Was she that unnoticeable? Did Duncan's words hold any meaning?

"No, no. You misunderstand. I only meant …" Lucas trailed off.

Selina wrenched herself out of his grip and hobbled over to a nearby bench. "Please, my lord, let us always have honesty between us, if not anything else."

"Are you hurt?"

"More than you can imagine," Selina mumbled.

Lucas helped lower her onto the bench. "I beg your pardon?"

Selina sighed. "I am fine. I only turned my ankle trying to keep pace with you."

Lucas slumped next to her. "Another fault to lay at my feet. It appears I am having a troublesome time of late on where I can step."

Selina didn't respond. How could she? Lucas made it more than clear he found her company lacking. He couldn't even remember he was walking with her in the garden.

Lucas turned toward her. "Selina, you spoke of us having honesty between us. Can we discuss our betrothal?"

Selina panicked. An eerie sensation came over her. Lucas wished to back out. She couldn't allow him to. "Will you kiss me?"

Lucas reeled back. "Excuse me?"

"Will you kiss me? Do you not wonder if we will be compatible in our marital bed? Is there any passion between us?" Each question held more desperation than the last.

Lucas jumped up and paced farther away from Selina. "What you ask is most improper. I cannot. No. No, I cannot."

Selina rose and stepped in front of him, resting her palms on his chest. When he didn't push her away, she pressed herself closer. Her fingers slid up and down on the lapels of his suit coat. She tilted her head up and caught his gaze. His eyes reflected what she felt. No spark of attraction, only discomfort at their position. Still, Selina must try to persuade him from breaking away from her. A small part of her wanted to prove Duncan wrong too. That need pushed her to stand on her tiptoes and press her lips against Lucas's.

Lucas gave Selina no reaction, remaining still. If Selina didn't have her hands upon him and feel his warmth, she would wonder if she didn't kiss a statue. His lips were cold and unresponsive. Yet Selina persisted, sliding her tongue along his lips. When he tried to object to the kiss, she slipped her tongue inside his mouth and stroked it along with his. Her own body tried to resist her actions, her mind screaming of its betrayal toward Duncan. The same gentleman who had forced her into this very act. Why wouldn't Lucas return her kiss? If only he would, then Selina would have proof of Duncan's lies, and it would give her the determination to follow through with the wedding.

While Selina fought with her doubts, Lucas took over the kiss. He gathered her closer and claimed her mouth as his. Selina almost hyperventilated at his reaction. Even though she'd started kissing him, her deepest thoughts had convinced her that he would never respond. It was the only reason she'd tried. She believed he would push her away in the end.

Now he deepened the kiss, each stroke of his trying to dance with hers. However, Selina no longer wanted any part of the dreaded kiss. She only wanted it to end. The only point it proved was how incompatible they were. No passion, but an awkwardness she wanted to forget.

Lucas pulled away from the kiss and stared into her eyes with an intentness that frightened Selina. "Yes, my dear, that was an excellent idea. We should have kissed sooner."

~~~~~

Duncan walked into the drawing room with Charlie on his arm. She soon moved away to join her husband. Duncan surveyed the room, noting Lucas and Selina were gone. Abigail stood outside on the terrace, staring into the garden. Duncan walked to her side and rested against the balustrade.

"They went for their walk in the garden," said Abigail forlornly.

Duncan sighed. "I know."

"Selina appeared upset after she gathered her shawl."

"I confess, another fault of mine."

"You are pushing her into his arms," Abigail whispered.

Duncan gripped Abigail's hand. "I am sorry, Abigail. It was not my intent. Jealousy reared its ugly head."

"It is ironic how I have become friends with Selina. But times like now, I still want to scratch her eyes out."

Duncan nodded. "Yes, she has that tendency about her. You may see her kind heart, but you do not dare turn your back on her."

"She only acts in that regard when someone has hurt her feelings and they provoked her to protect herself."

"How long have they been gone?"

"Too long."

Duncan offered his arm. "Then shall we take a stroll in the garden ourselves?"

A smile ghosted across Abigail's lips. "A walk will feel very refreshing, my lord."

Duncan chuckled. "Then right this way, my lady."

Duncan and Abigail walked down the stairs and into the garden. While his argument with Selina stayed fresh in his mind, he found common ground with Abigail, soothing his battered ego. They both suffered from loving people out of their grasp. Soon he had Abigail laughing over his antics at the last card game he'd played. But her laughter soon stopped, as did her steps. When she gasped loudly, he realized the source of her attention. There, standing but a few feet away, was Selina, wrapped in Lucas's embrace. Their heads were bent together, and they shared a kiss.

A kiss he drove Selina to with his accusations. A kiss he was to blame for provoking her into believing no one wanted her. A kiss that ripped his soul into shreds.

A kiss he despised.

A blaze of hatred coursed through his body. He hated the simple token of affection. He released Abigail's arm and stormed over to Selina and Lucas. His cousin's words to Selina of how excellent it was that they'd kissed pushed Duncan over the edge. He pulled them apart and slammed his fist into Lucas's gut. While Lucas grabbed at his stomach, Duncan swung his fist upward and clipped Lucas on the chin, sending him sprawling backward.

"What in the hell!" Lucas yelled.

"Duncan, how dare you!" Selina shouted.

He advanced on Lucas to finish pounding out his aggravation, but Abigail pulled at his arm. "Duncan, please stop," Abigail begged.

The heartbroken plea in her voice stopped him in his tracks. Duncan's crazed stare swung around, taking in each person. The misery in Abigail's gaze resonated in him, and he nodded at her. She released his arm, turned, and fled before he could offer her comfort.

When he swung his gaze to Selina, he watched her face transform as it did before. Every emotion he made her feel reflected in her eyes. But in the end, disappointment settled over her. She closed her eyes, shaking her head. Then she yelled after Abigail, following her out of the garden.

He wanted to chase after her again, but it was pointless. Selina had made her decision, and he must respect it, no matter how much it tore his heart apart. At Lucas's groan, Duncan turned toward his cousin and offered his hand. Lucas gripped it, and Duncan helped him to his feet. They both fell onto the bench.

Duncan leaned forward with his elbows on his knees. "I am sorry."

"It was to be expected."

Duncan looked at Lucas with confusion. "How so?"

Lucas threw his head back and sprawled out. "I heard footsteps and knew someone would come upon us. When I saw it was Abigail and you, I reacted, hoping to draw a reaction from Abigail. I used Selina for my own selfish means."

"I should punch you again," Duncan snarled.

Lucas nodded in agreement. "However, I was unprepared for your reaction. I thought perhaps you only fooled with Selina on my part. Not for your own reasons."

Duncan dropped his head into his hands. "At first, I found amusement riling her, then my feelings for the lass turned."

"When?"

"During the house party. What am I to do?"

"What are we both to do? We each care for a lady not meant for us. My father more than made his point clear on who I am to wed."

Duncan leaned back against the bench. "I cannot watch you marry Selina and spend your lives together. No offense, cousin, but you would make her miserable. I fear I spoke out of line with her earlier this evening and elicited her wrath."

Lucas laughed. "No offense taken. And I believe Selina shall forgive you. After all, she has forgiven all of your past offenses."

"Mmm." Duncan thought over Lucas's comment. There was some truth to it.

"I admit I hoped my lack of attention and cold indifference to her would have prompted her to call off the wedding, but Father ruined that by forcing me to attend to her every need. So I switched tactics, smothering her with my attention. I thought it was working too."

"How so?"

"Oh, she acted the polite lady, agreeing with whatever I said, and her manners were impeccable. However, when she thought I was not looking, she cringed whenever I drew near or touched her."

"You touched her?" Duncan growled.

Lucas's smile widened. "Easy, mate. 'Tis only when I offered her my arm or assistance of any kind. When I asked Selina to take a walk with me after this evening's dinner, she offered me a brittle smile and forced an answer of 'I would love to, my lord.' Then I managed to offend her during our walk. She threw me with her request to kiss her, and I acted out of spitefulness to hurt Abigail because of her stubbornness."

"And I am to blame for the kiss. I told Selina you only spent time with her under force. That you held no desire to kiss her, let alone to wed her."

"Why would you do that?"

"The green-eyed monster of jealousy urged me to."

Lucas's bitter laughter filled the garden. "You really are a Scottish heathen."

"I'd rather be one of those than a British stickler."

Lucas punched Duncan in the arm. "I am not."

Duncan laughed. "Oh, yes, you are, cousin. 'Tis why you still find yourself stuck in this madness."

Lucas narrowed his gaze. "There is no other way out."

Duncan arched his brow. "Is there not?"

"We would be mad to even attempt it."

Duncan shrugged. "I am game, if you are."

"I am. Who should go first?"

A devilish smirk spread across Duncan's face. "Oh, please allow me the pleasure."

Chapter Twenty

Selina chased after Abigail, only to lose her at the house. When she reached the steps leading to the terrace, her shoe slipped off her foot, and Selina was forced to stop. By the time she looked up, Abigail had disappeared.

Selina continued toward the drawing room to find only the younger guests remained. They gathered around the table playing cards, not paying Selina any attention. She took advantage of their disinterest and continued to her bedroom. When she reached the first landing, she heard male laughter coming from the billiard room. A billow of smoke escaped into the hallway when she glanced toward it.

Selina knew she would find her father involved in the gentlemen's entertainments. He enjoyed a steady flow of alcohol and the betting involved with pool, a pastime he only indulged in at house parties. Otherwise, he kept his vices limited, so as not to portray himself as a gentleman who held corrupt habits and squandered away his wealth. After all, he was a duke, and a duke and his family must portray themselves above all others as superior beings.

She continued until she reached Abigail's bedchamber. She knocked on the door quietly. "Abigail, please answer. I must speak with you."

No reply came, and Selina tried again. "It is not what it seems. Please, let me explain."

She pressed her forehead against the door, waiting for Abigail to open it. Abigail's crying seeped through the door, and guilt washed over Selina. She'd caused her new friend heartache. And for what reason? All because she'd reacted to her battered emotions without thinking of the consequences of her actions. In her effort to prove Duncan wrong, she'd hurt Abigail.

Not wanting to draw anyone's notice, Selina left Abigail to her own grief. She trudged along to her room and settled on the chaise. Selina curled on her side, looking out the window. Her gaze traveled over the estate, staring at nothing in particular. She kept playing the evening over and over. Each time her thoughts drifted to the kiss she shared with Lucas, and she saw how the fault lay with her. She rose and sat behind the small desk, pulling out a piece of paper. With her sorrow reflecting in her apology, Selina penned the first letter of this visit. She hoped she had grown from having to write these, but it appeared her insecurities still ruled her actions.

Dearest Abigail,

I did a foolish, foolish thing. I never intended to hurt you, but I did so with my selfish act. To prove Duncan's comments false, I lured Lucas into kissing me. Never imagining you would witness the kiss. I am so confused. I thought if Duncan learned of the kiss, he would stop his demands for having me call off the wedding, which leads to my other foolish act. I encouraged Duncan over the last two weeks, leading him to believe we had a future when only I used him to capture a brief moment of happiness for myself. Now, I have made all of our lives miserable with no escape. I wish you could help me with this dilemma I have found myself in.

Hopefully still your friend,

Selina

When her maid appeared, Selina turned the letter over. She would burn this letter like all the others tomorrow morning. The maid helped undress her for the night. Once she dismissed the maid, Selina crawled into bed and curled into a ball. It was then, and only then, that she allowed her own tears to fall. She cried for everything she'd loved and lost.

Friendship, acceptance, a sense of family, but most of all, love.

~~~~~

Meanwhile, Duncan strode through the manor with confidence. He was about to declare his love for Selina, and no one would stop him from loving her. Least of all his uncle. He reached Uncle Theo's study to find him entertaining his mother and father. That was perfect. His parents needed to learn of his intentions too.

He stepped inside, and their conversation ceased. He took in his mother's surprise and blush. His father relaxed in a chair with an amused expression on his face, and his uncle puffed away on his cigar, arching a brow at his intrusion.

"What can we do for you, my boy?" asked Colebourne.

Duncan closed the door for privacy. While everyone would soon learn of his declaration, he didn't want Selina's father to overhear until he confessed his love to Selina on bended knee, apologizing until she forgave him.

Duncan stepped in front of them, standing proud. "I love Selina and I plan to marry her. She will pledge her life to me and no other."

Colebourne narrowed his gaze. "Is that so?"

Duncan pinched his lips. "Yes." He would offer no other argument.

Colebourne laughed. "You think you can waltz into my study, make your declaration, and I will accept it with no questions asked?"

"You may ask all you want. But I offer no explanation except to the woman I love."

"And is she aware of your intentions?"

"No, but she soon will be."

Colebourne rose. "No, she will not. For you will not declare your love. Her marriage to Lucas has been set for years. I will not allow your simple infatuation to rip apart what I have built for Lucas and the future heirs of my dynasty."

"You would force the very people you care about to spend their lives in misery? All for what? Prestige? Honor? Money? Power? That is not love you feel, but greed," Duncan snarled.

Colebourne chuckled. "What do you know about honor? You betrayed your cousin for your latest amusement."

"Theo, that is enough!" Susanna exclaimed.

Ramsay placed his hand on his wife's arm. "No, Susanna. Let Colebourne say his piece. He speaks the truth. Duncan is the one who stepped over the bounds of propriety while playing with Lady Selina's emotions."

"I did not play with her emotions, nor is she my latest amusement. What do none of you understand? Selina is the love of my life! I will do everything in my power to save her from a marriage of suffering."

Colebourne cackled. "She will not suffer married to Lucas."

"That day will never happen," Duncan threatened. "I can promise you that."

Duncan turned and stormed out of the study, with his mother calling after him. He never responded to her, only walked deeper into the house to get away from the arrogance of his uncle's gaze. Not to mention the betrayal of his own father. When he reached his bedroom, he found Lucas sitting by the fire, holding a bottle of whiskey out to him.

"I thought you could use a drink. How did it go?"

Duncan drank a long swallow from the bottle. "As to be expected."

"What is your next step?"

Duncan shrugged. "I think I will finish this bottle. It would be a shame to waste such a fine whiskey."

Lucas laughed. "That it would."

For the first time in a long while, Duncan enjoyed the moment with his cousin. Lucas wasn't only a cousin, but a trusted mate. One he'd betrayed because of a fair-haired lass who had captured his heart with her vulnerability. It was no excuse, but then one must never apologize for love. Love was a rarity, a gift to be cared for and treasured above all else.

"I never meant to betray you."

Lucas shook his head. "You did no such thing. I find comfort in your love for Selina. I must confess to you my plans. Before the wedding took place, I planned to leave. I never wanted to hurt Selina, but you are correct. We would have made each other miserable. Now I can watch her marry someone who will love her with everything she is worth."

"You planned to leave? Your absence would have angered your father, not to mention Norbury. Why would you shame Selina with your selfishness?" Duncan growled.

"So you could step in like a gallant hero and marry her for yourself. Norbury cannot take a stand against being robbed. Hell, your holdings outweigh mine. Everyone would win. My father will have fulfilled his end of the bargain, Norbury can strut around London with his newfound power, your parents will be in high heaven over the match, and Selina will have married the gentleman who captured her heart."

"You thought of everything. Even sneaking your way out of your commitment. You are as devious as your father. I am most impressed."

"It is a plan of madness. I only hope it will achieve its outcome. Even though you declared your intentions to my father, he will still demand I wed Selina. I will disappear before the wedding, leaving you to fill my position for the ruined event."

Duncan thought the plan over. "It might work."

"It will."

"And what of Abigail?"

Lucas took a deep breath. "The same as it always has been. My father has a suitor for her. You know my position. I cannot marry beneath my station. Nor is it proper since she is my father's ward."

"Bollocks."

Lucas arched a brow at the slanderous word.

"Do not give me your practiced ducal stare. Your excuses are rubbish. When will you declare your love for the poor lass?"

Lucas stood. "Never."

Duncan watched his cousin leave without saying another word. He let him leave with his determination. Lucas could fool himself all he wanted, but in time, the madness would overcome him too.

Only then would he succumb to love.

~~~~~~

"Oh, this match is playing out perfectly. Your boy has such passion for the lass." Colebourne cackled.

"You were a little harsh with him, were you not?" Susanna asked disapprovingly.

Ramsay joined in with Colebourne's laughter. "No, his conceit was spot on. The boy is so rattled he does not even realize it."

Susanna turned to her husband, frowning. "You were no better toward him."

"Ah, it was just what the boy needed. I can now understand your enjoyment with this matchmaking business. I might extend my visit to help with the next match. How about we make Duncan and Selina's match more interesting?"

Colebourne's smile turned wicked. "What do you have in mind?"

Ramsay rubbed his hands together. "I bet fifty quid he tries to run off with the bride to Scotland."

Colebourne's grin turned cocky. "Make it one hundred. And he marries her in the local village because my son runs away on the big day."

Ramsay stood up and shook Colebourne's hand. "You have a deal. Now come, my dear, I must work on my speech to welcome Selina into our family."

Susanna grabbed Ramsay's hand, tsking at their deal. Colebourne watched the loving couple leave, with Susanna exclaiming her delight in gaining Selina for a daughter. He put out his cigar and crossed the room to pour himself a shot of whiskey. He moved before the fireplace and stared at the portrait above the mantle.

"I promise you, my dear Olivia, I only acted with the best of my heart. Selina and Lucas would have lived in misery because they love other souls. Selina and Duncan share a passionate love, and Lucas loves Abigail, who also loves him. Of that I am sure. They will come together soon, my love."

He toasted his late wife, downing the fiery liquid as he drank in the beauty of his soul mate. A smile of satisfaction spread across his face at another love match he'd made.

Only two more to go.

Chapter Twenty-One

Selina awoke refreshed, ready to battle the day. Throughout the night of tossing and turning, she thought over her dilemma and decided no one would determine the course of her fate.

She stood before the mirror, gazing at herself. When choosing her outfit, she decided on a simple day dress. It wasn't appropriate for her station, but she felt comfortable in it. It wasn't even one she should wear to hold an audience with a duke, let alone two dukes. Selina smiled as she remembered her maid's shock at the unassuming garment. It was one she wore while toiling in the garden. Yet, another activity her father issued a forbiddance on, but one she snuck around to do. If she planned to defend her stand, then she would seek comfort where she could.

All her life, Selina's father had preached about the elevation of her station and what he expected of her. As the daughter of a duke, it was her duty to marry a duke's firstborn son. Even Selina fooled herself into believing she wanted the same outcome. It wasn't until she'd opened her eyes to the dynamics of how a friendship worked and watched how a loving family treated one another that she saw matters differently. The final eye-opener was the passion she shared with the man who held her heart.

When she kissed Lucas, it was the act of a desperate soul clinging to a fantasy she never truly wanted, but it'd been the only one she had only ever known. Now Selina understood the possibilities before her if only she opened herself to them. But before she could explore what life held for her, she must break the bonds holding her within its grasp.

Selina left her room, taking in the closed doors along the hallway. By now, the other ladies had joined each other for their morning ritual. They thought to confuse her by keeping their doors closed. Selina hoped to rectify the situation with her confession. She made her way to the duke's study and knocked. The duke bid her to enter, and she noticed her father sat across the desk from Colebourne. This was perfect. She would confront them together.

Colebourne rose from his seat and came around the desk to greet Selina. "Good morning, my dear. Your father and I were finalizing the marital agreement. What may I do for you?"

"I would like a private word with you and my father concerning the marriage, if I may?"

Colebourne indicated the chair next to her father. "Yes. Please take a seat."

Selina sat down and glanced at her father. His frown spoke volumes. But she wouldn't allow him to intimidate her. "Thank you."

"Selina, this matter does not concern you." Her father's voice held a warning, one she chose to ignore.

"I disagree, Norbury. 'Tis her life." Colebourne nodded for Selina to speak.

Selina sat up straighter in her chair, holding her hands tightly together in her lap. "There is a clause in the agreement stating I may withdraw from the contract. Is this correct?"

"Yes, you are correct. Lucas is aware of the clause. I only assumed you were too," answered Colebourne.

"Selina!" Norbury barked.

Selina raised her chin with determination. "Then I withdraw my name. In good conscience, I cannot marry Lucas. Another gentleman has stolen my heart, and I have given him my virtue. I have no clue if he will offer for my hand. I will only marry him if he professes his love and asks because he chooses to, not because someone has forced him to."

Colebourne leaned against the desk, observing Selina with shrewdness. "Your actions take much courage. I applaud you for following your heart. By all good faith, I must accept your withdrawal, much to my disappointment, for you would have made an endearing daughter-in-law. But my late wife and your mother made this a stipulation in the contract, and I will honor their request."

"My mother?"

Colebourne smiled. "Yes, dear. She loved you dearly and protected you with her heart. She only wanted the best for you, and I believe you have found the best in the gentleman who holds your heart."

Norbury stood in a rage. "I object. She is not in her right mind. Just like her foolish mother, she believes in fantasies. A rogue's promise has filled her head with tales. Selina will follow through on her commitment to wed Gray. I will stand for nothing less. And I will have this reprobate's name so I can destroy him for ruining my daughter."

Colebourne rose to his full height, towering over Norbury by a few inches, and glared at him. "The marriage contract is now void upon Selina's confession. As for her not being in her right mind, I believe she finally has the confidence to capture her dreams. And you will not ruin her chance at happiness. If you even think of destroying the gentleman she loves, then he will have my backing to ruin you in return."

"You have not heard the end of my argument on this matter, Colebourne." Norbury looked at Selina with disgust. "As for you, you are no longer my daughter. I disown you. For your sake, I hope your lover offers for your hand. If he does not, then your situation will crumble around you, taking a turn you are unprepared for. You shall not receive another coin from me," he snarled before stalking out of the study.

Selina stared at her hands clenched tightly on her lap, too embarrassed to face Colebourne. She had prepared herself for her father's brutal words and his abandonment. However, his reaction still pierced her heart. But his cruelty didn't change her mind. It only strengthened her determination to make her own decisions for her future.

"Selina?"

Selina raised her head.

Colebourne offered her a comforting smile. "You were very brave, my dear, to take a stand. For a while there, you scared me. I did not think you would dare."

Selina looked confused. "I do not understand."

"I have known for quite a while of your affair with Duncan."

Selina blushed a bright red. "I … uh …"

Colebourne chuckled. "Do not fret. I quite approve." He winked at her. "One might even say I helped encourage it along. However, the betrothal agreement tied my hands. Only you or Lucas could break the contract. So when Duncan confronted me last night of his undying love for you and his refusal to allow the wedding to happen, I hoped you would soon profess of your own love for him."

"He loves me?"

"Yes," Colebourne reassured Selina's doubt.

Selina pinched her lips. "He has not told me so. I believe he holds an infatuation toward me, but 'tis all."

"Perhaps he is waiting to make a grand gesture to declare his love. After all, the boy is a romantic."

"I have yet to witness romance where Duncan Forrester is concerned," Selina scoffed.

Colebourne threw back his head, and his boisterous laughter filled the air. "Oh, your union with my nephew will be a joy to watch in the years to come."

"If he offers."

"Oh, he will, my dear. However, for now, why not visit your friends in the village today? I am positive they would love to see you again. It will help take your mind off the drama unfolding in this household."

Selina's smile turned bittersweet. "Do you not mean to take myself away to escape my father's wrath?"

Colebourne helped Selina rise and walked her toward the door. "It is probably for the best. I will try to reason with him. If I cannot, then you must understand you are now part of my family, no matter what becomes of the outcome of your decision."

"Thank you, Your Grace."

He patted Selina's hand and winked again. "Uncle Theo."

Selina's smile brightened. "Uncle Theo."

Colebourne watched Selina walk up the stairs to her bedchamber. He ordered the footman standing nearby to gather Lucas, Duncan, Ramsay, and his cohort in this matchmaking business, Susanna, to his study immediately. They needed to pull off a marriage ceremony before Norbury interfered. Then he informed his butler to find whatever means necessary to keep Norbury away from Selina until she spoke her vows to Duncan.

~~~~~~~

Selina hurried to her room. Before her father cornered her with his threats, she would take Colebourne's advice to visit Anna and her friends in the village. After she grabbed her bonnet and changed shoes, she would be on her way.

Selina stepped over the threshold and came to a halt. Abigail stood by the desk, reading the letter Selina had written the night before.

"Oh, no," Selina gasped, realizing she had forgotten to burn the note.

Abigail raised her head at Selina's gasp and dropped the letter, backing away from the desk. "Gemma asked for me to collect her stationary. I never meant…"

"I moved it to the bottom drawer."

Abigail pointed at the missive. "Why did you write me a letter?"

Blowing out a breath, Selina walked over to the desk and picked up the paper. "It is a habit I developed over the years. A way to offer my apologies for my shrewish behavior."

Abigail's gaze reflected her confusion. "Were you going to deliver it to me?"

Selina released a brittle laugh. "No. I never do. I burn them after I write them. The same fear of rejection that prompts my appalling behavior keeps me from delivering them."

"Have you written many?"

"More than I can count. For every act of cruelty I have dealt to every member of this family, I have written a letter apologizing for my behavior and seeking forgiveness."

"Oh, Selina. If only you had sent them, we would not have held onto our bitterness toward you."

Selina shrugged. "It was easier to keep with my vicious behavior. It helped to protect my heart."

"May I?" Abigail pointed to the letter.

Selina handed it over to her, and Abigail folded it, sliding it into her pocket. "I forgive you."

Selina's eyes widened. "You do?"

Abigail smiled kindly. "Yes. Friends forgive each other. Your letter explained your actions, and I understand. Duncan can provoke anyone into making rash mistakes. Now, you have asked for my help with your dilemma. How may I be of assistance?"

"Do you want to join me today? I am visiting a friend in the village."

"I would love to."

"We must hurry, then. I need to leave before my father finds me." Selina sat on the chaise and changed her shoes quickly, then gathered her bonnet.

"Are you in trouble?"

"Yes. I will explain on our walk." Selina started down the hallway with Abigail following slowly behind her.

"Perhaps we should leave after your father talks with you." Abigail hesitated. With her inferior position in society, she didn't want to endure a duke's wrath.

"I have no wish to speak with him, nor will I." Selina stopped outside Abigail's room. "Hurry, grab your bonnet."

Abigail sighed and did Selina's bidding. She gathered her bonnet and walked with Selina outdoors. Soon, they were trudging over the countryside toward a small group of cottages on Colebourne's land. Abigail was unaware of Selina's friendship with the ladies in question. Abigail had spent much time among them, sewing and playing with their children. She shook her head at their common interests and the wasted years they'd spent as enemies. They could have been friends all along.

Abigail stopped near a tree and sat down, refusing to walk another step until Selina explained their quick departure. "Selina, please slow down. We are far enough away that your father will not bother us."

Selina stopped and took a deep breath. When the stitch in her side started burning, Selina realized she'd kept them at a brisk pace. "I suppose you are correct." Selina sat next to Abigail, breathing heavily.

They sat in silence, each of them catching their breath. The slight panic Selina felt before she'd left the estate started suffocating her. While she remained confident about her decision to call off the wedding, her father's brutal words still bruised her heart. She refused to allow him to smother the relief coursing through her veins. She wanted her happiness to grow by leaps and bounds. Selina had endeared enough unhappiness in her lifetime.

"You can have Lucas," Selina blurted out.

Abigail whipped her head around, startled. "I do not want him."

"Please," Selina scoffed.

"I have no use for an arrogant arse who thinks I am below him. You can keep him."

Selina's smile widened at Abigail's bold declaration. "He is no longer mine because I have no use for him either."

"Yes, you do," Abigail insisted.

"No, I do not. I want his cousin instead."

"But you cannot. You are set to wed Lucas."

"Not anymore. I broke the betrothal this morning."

"How? Why?"

Selina laughed and leaned against the tree. "I confessed my love for another to Colebourne and asked him to release me from the contract. He informed me of a stipulation my mother and Lucas's mother demanded in the contract. The clause stated Lucas or I could break the contract for any reason."

"Does Lucas know of this clause?"

Selina observed Abigail, not wanting to hurt her feelings, but she needed to speak the truth. "Yes."

Sadness settled over Abigail. "Oh."

"Just because Lucas never attempted to break the betrothal, it does not reflect on his feelings for you. Our fathers placed us under the same pressure. His honor would not allow him to break a promise."

"Lucas only holds a responsibility toward me. 'Tis all."

Selina shook her head. "You are wrong. He cares deeply."

Abigail didn't respond to Selina's opinion. Her relationship with Lucas confused her without having to explain it to another. While her heart wished for Selina to be correct, reality proved otherwise. "Why then?"

"Because I did not wish to have a marriage based on misery. I want a marriage full of love. If I married him, I would continue to long for another, which would have been unfair to Lucas. I could not marry Lucas while loving Duncan. The bonds constricting my every move grew tiresome. My greatest wish is to feel the freedom of living my life by my choosing."

Abigail nodded in understanding. A silly grin settled over Selina's face, showcasing her sincere beauty. Abigail admired Selina for her bravery to stand up for herself. It was a rare occurrence for a lady to declare her intentions so boldly and to find acceptance. But were her actions accepted? "I assume with the need to put distance from your father, he objected to your decision?"

Selina's lips twisted. "With malice."

"And Colebourne?"

"With the grace of a true gentleman. He offered me his protection from my father and the use of his home until I am settled."

"Does Lucas know?"

"I assume Colebourne will inform him."

Abigail arched a brow. "And Duncan?"

Selina cringed. "No. I fear his rejection after the stunt I pulled in the garden."

"How can I help?"

Selina blushed. "I wish to sneak into his chambers with no one noticing."

Abigail laughed. "That will be easy enough. There is a secret passageway I can help you navigate."

Selina's blushed darkened. "I already know of it. However, there is a servant stationed in it."

Abigail's eyes widened. "There is? I wonder why?"

Selina shrugged, unsure herself.

"Well, then we shall just have to sneak you in unnoticed. You are in luck since Duncan did not bring a valet with him. Leave it to me. I will recruit Gemma to help."

"You will help me, even after I kissed Lucas?"

"We have moved past that incident, Selina. And I will take great pleasure in helping you and Duncan unite."

Selina threw her arms around Abigail, hugging her with enthusiasm. "Thank you, my friend."

Abigail returned Selina's hug before rising. She held her hand out. "Shall we visit your friends?"

"Yes, let us enjoy the day."

Selina and Abigail interlocked their arms and continued to Anna's cottage. Abigail explained her friendship with the ladies too. When they arrived, the children gathered around them, begging for stories, and the ladies smiled their gratitude for a few minutes of respite. Selina and Abigail played with the children and shared tea with the ladies. When they paid their goodbyes, they promised to bring treats on their next visit.

Selina finally felt her life falling into a place she'd only ever dreamed of. Now to convince a certain Scottish barbarian she loved him with all her heart.

Chapter Twenty-Two

Duncan paced up and down the stretch of the hallway. Each time, he paused at Selina's bedroom and glanced inside, thinking she'd magically appeared without his notice. He grew impatient for her return. Once she arrived, he planned to pledge his undying devotion to her. No. He should ask for her forgiveness first. No. Perhaps he should lead with how much he loved her? Yes, a much better option. He raked his hands through his hair, growing more agitated at Selina's absence.

It seemed like an eternity since his uncle had called him into his study, informing Duncan how Selina had broken the betrothal agreement. Uncle Theo had granted Duncan permission to pursue the blonde-haired beauty. Uncle Theo believed he'd navigated another successful match, and Duncan let him take the credit. Because without his underhanded maneuvering and turning a blind eye to Duncan's scandalous activities, Selina and Duncan might not have fallen in love.

He heard giggling coming from the staircase and strode to the landing, hoping it was Selina. Duncan released a breath he hadn't realized he held. Selina and Abigail trailed up the stairs, twirling their bonnets and laughing gaily. He tried to speak her name, but nothing came out. He'd never seen her looking so carefree and beautiful. A natural glow of happiness radiated from her. Duncan cleared his throat.

Selina paused on the stairs next to Abigail when she saw Duncan standing at the top of the staircase. He appeared nervous. His hair stood on end, and his hands kept moving on their own accord, not staying in one place too long before shifting to another position. However, his gaze froze Selina on the steps. Every emotion he felt for her radiated from him, leaving no need for him to utter a word.

The final weight of the unknown lifted from Selina's shoulders with his stare. She exclaimed with glee and ran up the steps, throwing herself in his arms. She needed no whispered words, pleads for forgiveness, or oaths of love. Selina only wanted Duncan to hold her in his arms and to place his lips upon hers. Duncan's kisses always made her feel whole.

Duncan was unprepared for the whirlwind flying into his arms. He grabbed the banister with one hand and wrapped her tightly with his other arm.

Abigail's laughter floated up to them, and her quip echoed. "I suppose we do not need our plan after all."

He looked at Abigail, but she had already disappeared back down the stairs.

Selina pressed kisses against his neck. "Please, forgive me."

Duncan twirled her around, pressing Selina against the railing. He cupped her cheek. "I wish to ask the same of you. But I already know you do. Uncle Theo told me what you did this morning. For me?"

Selina nodded, a smile beaming from her face. "Aye."

He pressed his forehead against hers, staring deeply into her eyes. "I love you, lass."

"You hold my heart, Duncan."

Duncan pressed a light kiss to her lips, but pulled away before she could deepen it. He growled, wanting to devour her. However, more important matters needed to be accomplished. "Do you trust me?"

"Yes."

"Will you marry me?"

Selina narrowed her gaze. "Is your uncle forcing your hand?"

Duncan threw his head back and laughed. He had ruined the lass. She had so much as admitted to it hours ago, and now she questioned how he would defend her honor. Only Selina would do so. "Nay."

"You are under no coercion?"

"No."

"Then yes."

"Yes?"

"Yes."

Duncan let out a yelp of excitement and swung Selina in circles along the hallway toward her bedchamber. He set Selina on her feet inside the room. She swayed from the dizziness, clutching his arm.

"I take it she answered yes?" Lady Forrester asked excitedly.

"Aye," Duncan answered his mother, smiling down at Selina.

"Then shoo, off with you. We have much to accomplish, as do you." Lady Forrester pulled him away and dragged him out the door.

"Until later, my love." Duncan blew her a kiss.

Selina giggled at his display of affection. She turned, and her gaze fell on her wedding dress hanging near the mirror. Surrounding the dress were Abigail, Jacqueline, Charlie, Evelyn, and Gemma. Each of them wore a silly grin of approval.

She turned toward Lady Forrester. "I do not understand."

Lady Forrester closed the door and snapped her fingers. Each lady jumped to attention and helped Selina disrobe. "You have a groom anxiously awaiting you at the altar."

By then they had stripped Selina down to her chemise and urged her toward a chair in front of the vanity. Gemma drew a brush through her hair and explained Selina's confusion away. "Uncle Theo secured a private license for you to wed Duncan before he left England."

"What? I came to Colebourne Manor to marry Lucas."

Charlie laughed. "That is what he chose for you to believe. But Uncle Theo knew Duncan would charm you into loving him."

"How?"

"By throwing you together at every opportunity he could without your father growing too suspicious," answered Evelyn.

"Then why force Lucas to spend time with me?"

"Ahh, that was his tactic to pull the strings of the parties involved to admit to their feelings." Gemma started weaving flowers through Selina's hair, leaving it hanging along her back.

"Once you and Duncan confessed your love for one another, Uncle Theo achieved the results he needed to make another successful match." Jacqueline helped Selina rise and guided her toward the pink creation.

Selina reached out to touch the soft fabric, remembering Duncan's reaction to seeing her in the dress. A blush stole across her cheeks. "Match?"

"Our uncle sees himself as a matchmaker. He chose you in his mad scheme to make a match with Duncan," said Evelyn.

"Why play his game with me when he held an agreement promising me to his son?"

Charlie laughed. "Mmm. The golden question. Why do we not ask his co-conspirator? Can you help answer Selina's question, Aunt Susanna?"

All eyes turned to Aunt Susanna. Her grin turned wicked at their question, then quickly smoothed into innocence. "You girls need to help Abigail dress. I will finish taking care of Selina." She brushed them out the door with no explanation before hurrying toward Selina.

Lady Forrester helped Selina dress and stood back, nodding in approval. She gathered Selina's hands in hers and smiled. "Ramsay and I wish to express our honor at welcoming you into our family with open arms. We wish you many years of happiness with Duncan. We could not be prouder of him for choosing you as a bride."

A tear trickled along Selina's cheek at her kind words. "Thank you, Lady Forrester."

"Perhaps Mother?" Lady Forrester asked hopefully.

"Mama?"

Lady Forrester wrapped Selina in her arms. "Mama."

Lady Forrester pulled away and helped Selina gather her gown over her arm. "Now we must hurry. We do not want to be late for your wedding."

"My father?"

Mama closed her eyes at Selina's question. "He has already departed for London." She opened her eyes, regarding Selina with sadness.

Selina gave her a bittersweet smile and nodded. She wouldn't cry over her father's departure. She'd received his message loud and clear, and she refused to allow him to control her happiness any longer. It saddened Selina that he wouldn't see her wed, but that was his choice, not hers.

With a new determination, Selina strode outdoors. She couldn't wait a second longer to become Duncan's bride. She'd dreaded this day for the past few weeks. Now she anxiously waited for it to become a reality. The only difference was the groom. She laughed at the madness of it all.

Her new mother helped her into the carriage, and they took off for the wedding destination. Colebourne had requested she marry Lucas on the grounds near the gazebo. Selina assumed her marriage to Duncan would take place at the same location. However, the carriage traveled past the destination. Selina wondered why they hadn't stopped. Before she could question it, their carriage ride ended. When the door swung open, Ramsay helped them step down.

Mama hustled inside, and Ramsay offered Selina his arm. "What do you say, lass? I hear ye be taking him off my hands."

Selina laughed. "Aye. Unless ye be wanting to keep him a bit longer."

Ramsay roared with amusement. "Nay. Ye can have him."

Selina smiled. "Will you walk me to my groom?"

Ramsay bussed her cheek. "With pleasure."

Ramsay led Selina inside the small village church. Colebourne and his family, along with her friends from the village, filled the pews. Candles lit the church in a soft glow, and Duncan stood waiting with the priest. He wore a kilt with his family's colors, along with a smug smile. Selina shook her head at his arrogance.

When Ramsay passed her over to him, Duncan whispered in her ear, "Do you remember when I stated how you would wear this gown for me?"

Selina nodded. She remembered it quite clearly. What he didn't know was that she'd chosen the gown while picturing him as her groom. Even though she'd prepared herself for a life of doom married to Lucas Gray, she still held out hope for Duncan. A secret she would share with him on one of their anniversaries. Heaven forbid she build his ego higher on their wedding day.

The ceremony and celebration were everything Selina imagined them to be and more. They ate a simple fare and danced late into the night. Colebourne hired local musicians to play for them. Selina danced with her groom to silly jigs and twirled around with the children. It couldn't have gone more perfectly. Even Lucas joined the celebration after a rumor spread of him fleeing. His guilty conscience forced him to return in time to join the celebration. Selina even caught him trying to persuade Abigail to dance, only for her to rebuff him and dance with a local squire instead. She chuckled at the refusal she witnessed.

When Duncan asked what struck her amusement, she whispered, "'Tis nothing at all," before kissing her groom.

Duncan stole her away in a carriage before the party ended. They traveled for an hour before stopping at an inn tucked away from the regular road. When they reached their room, rose petals decorated the floor and bed, and a bottle of chilled champagne rested on the nightstand. The warmth of the fireplace filled the space, and candles decorated the room in a glow. A romantic setting for their wedding night. How much more perfect could her groom be?

Selina turned toward Duncan and slid her hands around his neck, pulling his head down for a kiss. It wasn't a sweet kiss, but one full of promises for an evening of sinful pleasures. Not a kiss of a chaste bride, timid to become his wife, but one of a confident wife who wanted to claim her husband. When Duncan tried to deepen the kiss, Selina pulled away and went to work on the buttons of his shirt. He had discarded his cravat and suit coat while they danced.

Once she undid the last button, she dragged it over his head and admired his firm chest and brawny arms. A chest she would spend every night lying upon while his arms held her during their sleep.

However, sleep was the furthest thing from her mind this evening.

Selina worked on the bindings to his kilt and watched as it dropped to the floor. Her husband stood proud in all his glory. His cocky grin beckoned her to finish what she'd started. She set her hands on his chest and ran them down to his thighs, her hand softly brushing across his hardness before bringing them back up again. A fire of need replaced his cockiness at her touch. He trapped her hands against his chest before she teased him again.

"Do not tease me tonight, lass. 'Tis not a wise course to take."

A sinful smile graced her lips. "Perhaps I do not tease."

Duncan arched a brow. "Selina," he warned.

Selina dropped to her knees and pressed a kiss against his hardness. She wished to pleasure him, but he kept a hold of her hands, clenching them to his heart. Which left Selina only one option. Her tongue circled the tip of his cock, guiding him into her mouth. His groan echoed around the room. Selina slid her mouth down the length of him, drawing him in deeper. Her tongue swirled around, savoring the taste of Duncan.

It took everything in Duncan's power to stay upright. His knees begged to buckle at the onslaught of Selina's passion. Her mouth tortured him with its demands. Each lick and stroke of her tongue sent him reeling with a need out of his control. His body demanded its release. Her love undid him. Her fingers stayed relaxed in his grasp. If she so much as touched him, he would lose control.

Selina moaned as Duncan's body shook. His need reflected her own. She wanted Duncan to make her his wife. She pulled her mouth away and rose again. "Are you going to fulfill your promise of taking me in this dress?"

The passion in Duncan's growl vibrated against their joined hands. "Aye."

He picked Selina up and threw her over his shoulder, striding toward the chaise in the corner. She laughed and pounded on his back. "Must you be a Scottish barbarian on our wedding night?"

Duncan sat on the chaise, drawing Selina to straddle his lap. "Aye. And you wish for me to act no other way. Am I correct, lass?"

Selina moaned when Duncan's hand traveled under her skirt. "Aye."

Duncan's hand paused when he reached her core. "Selina?"

"Mmm."

"I." His hand brushed across her wetness. "Love." He slid a finger inside her, stroking her inside and out. "You." His thumb pressed across her clit, bringing forth a pleasurable moan.

Selina threw her head back, arching her chest toward Duncan's mouth. Her body craved to feel his lips upon hers. When he pulled his hands away, Selina whimpered her displeasure. Before she could voice them, he lifted her and thrust inside her.

"Ohhh, my."

She came down upon him and clung to his shoulders, staring into his wicked eyes. He pressed into her again, and Selina's eyelids fluttered at the exquisite act. His tongue trailed across her chest, caressing her slowly, making Selina ache. She opened her heavy lids to watch him dip his tongue into the valley of her breasts. She moaned, pressing herself closer to him.

Their eyes clashed, and the desire burning between them pushed Selina over.

"Duncan!" Selina screamed.

Duncan gripped her waist and sent Selina reeling all over again each time he pressed up into her. Selina's ache intensified. She moved her body with each of his strokes, clinging to him.

Selina came undone over and over each time he slid in deeper. He couldn't take his eyes off her. She glowed from his loving. His body begged to follow her, but he craved so much more from her. Each stroke grew bolder, and she matched him, swaying in motion with him. Selina's wetness clenched around him, clinging with her need. Duncan succumbed to the pleasure and came undone with Selina toward the bliss of ecstasy.

She was his world. His every fantasy turned to reality. A dream come true. Every cliché a man declared about the woman he loved.

He took her lips in a kiss, expressing the emotions his soul couldn't speak. A slow kiss filled with devotion. A kiss of love.

The emotions coursing through Selina's soul expressed themselves in the form of tears. She couldn't stop them from spilling forth. Duncan's kiss spoke of his love. She needed no words from him, for his every action declared his genuine emotions. He kissed her tears away, needing no explanation as to why she cried. Duncan was now her home.

He gathered her closer. Their love surrounded them while their hearts slowed to beat as one. Even when he thought he'd lost her, he never gave up hope for them. No words were needed on how they had become husband and wife today. The years they would share in happiness would show proof. Still, he needed to express his love.

"I love you with all my heart, Duchess."

"And I love you, my Scottish barbarian."

Selina pressed a soft kiss against his lips before snuggling into him. She didn't care what had led to their marriage. None of it mattered. Duncan loved her, and they would enjoy a lifetime together. His family joked about Colebourne's matchmaking madness, but Selina owed her gratitude for the duke's schemes.

If not, she wouldn't have found the loving embrace of her husband.

Epilogue

Duncan watched his wife play with the children during the village's celebration of St. Andrew's Day. His mother sat nearby, holding his cousin's bairn on her lap. He hoped she would hold his own soon. A pleasure he tried for every night with his wife.

"Ye must tell her now, son. Your cousins will not keep it quiet on their visit. It has been unfair of you to ask it of your mother and me," Ramsay told him.

Duncan sighed. "I know I must tell her. I thank ye for it. However, with granddad's arrival upon us, I must confess my secret."

Ramsay nodded toward Selina. "Best do it now."

Duncan started toward Selina. He hated to ruin her day, but his grandfather was due to arrive soon to meet Selina and give his approval. If Duncan didn't admit to his slight omission, and she learned of his wealth by another means, he would suffer a rift in their marriage, and that was one he never wanted.

However, Selina felt such a sense of relief at not becoming a duchess. She admitted how much she'd dreaded the social aspect of it since she struggled to find common interests with her peers. However, all had changed. Selina had grown into herself, relaxed with whomever she met, and easily made friends. She told him it was from not having the pressure of society watching her.

In the two months since their wedding, they'd stayed at his parents' estate, enjoying the holiday with his Scottish relatives. Now, with Christmas almost upon them, his grandfather came to visit. Soon, Colebourne and his clan would descend on them for the month. His mother and Uncle Theo still had one more match to make. Shortly after they departed for their honeymoon, Jacqueline had wed, which only left Lucas and Abigail at the mercy of their matchmaking madness.

"Duncan, please dance with us." Selina twirled around him in a circle.

Duncan chuckled at her childlike behavior. "I would love to, my dear. However, there is a matter I must discuss with you."

Selina paused at the seriousness in Duncan's tone. She frowned when he shifted on his feet, nervously glancing at his mother. When Mama rose with the bairn and guided the children away, Selina realized Mama knew what Duncan wished to discuss, and she didn't wish to stick around.

"Very well, husband. Shall we take a walk?"

Duncan nodded. They started off, but when they reached a nestle of trees, he stopped and guided Selina to a bench he'd set up nearby.

Selina folded her hands in her lap. "What is so dire?"

Duncan sat beside her and laid his hand over hers. "Do you promise to let me explain after I tell you, Duchess?"

"I told you how much I loathe that name," she scolded him.

Duncan winced. "Even if it holds some truth?"

Selina scoffed. "Thankfully, not any longer."

"And if the truth plays out in the distant future?"

Selina laughed. "Not likely, my dear. In which I express my gratitude to you daily. I wish for no other life than what we have created with your parents."

"And we can still have that. However, once my grandfather passes away, I will become a *duke*, therefore making you a *duchess*," Duncan rambled off quickly before he lost his nerve.

Selina tried pulling her hand away, but he kept a firm hold. "I beg your pardon?"

Duncan sighed. "My mother's father is a duke. Since he only had two daughters, the line fell to their offspring. Since I was born before Lucas, my grandfather's dukedom and all his holdings will fall to me."

"How would I not know of this?"

"My grandfather lives in northern Scotland and prefers it to his holdings in England. He pays us a visit to meet you."

Selina sat, shock crossing over her features at this bit of knowledge. It should make sense to her now. The comments made to her about his wealth before they spoke their wedding vows, her father's sudden forgiveness, and how his cousins kept calling her Duchess. Selina thought they only teased her, but now she would understand the full brunt of her husband's secrecy.

She pasted on a fake smile. "Thank you for informing me of your wealth and status in society. I am sorry I misjudged you." She escaped from his grasp and stalked away.

Duncan jumped up and followed her inside their cottage. She said nothing else, only tidying the small space. Then suddenly she came upon him and thumped him on the chest. "You are not only a Scottish barbarian, but a deceitful brute. How dare you subject me to lies in our marriage?"

"I am sorry. Please, forgive me."

"Did you fool me for revenge? Because I stated you were not worthy of my attention."

"No. I swear. I think of my wealth as unimportant. Then you displayed your happiness, carrying on about how ecstatic you were to be free from the pressures of society. I cringed at taking away your joy until I had to."

Duncan paced back and forth, explaining his reasons, one after another. And the entire time Selina's smile kept spreading at his groveling. Before long, she roared with laughter.

Duncan swung toward her, his gaze narrowing at her amusement. "You knew."

"Aye."

"For how long?"

"A wee bit after we settled in the cottage," Selina attempted to answer in her Scottish accent she'd yet to perfect.

"Why, you Scottish heathen!" He advanced on her and threw her over his shoulder.

Selina's giggles filled the small cottage until her screams of pleasure shook the rafters. Never underestimate a lady in love who wanted to learn everything she could about her husband. And never underestimate a Scot who would do anything to ensure his bride's happiness.

And most importantly, never underestimate the power of love.

Look for Jacqueline's story in October 2021!

If you would like to hear my latest news then visit my website www.lauraabarnes.com to join my mailing list.

"Thank you for reading How the Scot Stole the Bride. Gaining exposure as an independent author relies mostly on word-of-mouth, so if you have the time and inclination, please consider leaving a short review wherever you can."

Author Laura A. Barnes

International selling author Laura A. Barnes fell in love with writing in the second grade. After her first creative writing assignment, she knew what she wanted to become. Many years went by with Laura filling her head full of story ideas and some funny fish songs she wrote while fishing with her family. Thirty-seven years later, she made her dreams a reality. With her debut novel *Rescued By the Captain*, she has set out on the path she always dreamed about.

When not writing, Laura can be found devouring her favorite romance books. Laura is married to her own Prince Charming (who for some reason or another thinks the heroes in her books are about him) and they have three wonderful children and two sweet grandbabies. Besides her love of reading and writing, Laura loves to travel. With her passport stamped in England, Scotland, and Ireland; she hopes to add more countries to her list soon.

While Laura isn't very good on the social media front, she loves to hear from her readers. You can find her on the following platforms:

You can visit her at *www.lauraabarnes.com* to join her mailing list.

Website: **http://www.lauraabarnes.com**
Amazon: **https://amazon.com/author/lauraabarnes**
Goodreads: **https://www.goodreads.com/author/show/16332844.Laura_A_Barnes**
Facebook: **https://www.facebook.com/AuthorLauraA.Barnes/**
Instagram: **https://www.instagram.com/labarnesauthor/**
Twitter: **https://twitter.com/labarnesauthor**
BookBub: **https://www.bookbub.com/profile/laura-a-barnes**

Desire more books to read by Laura A. Barnes

Enjoy these other historical romances:

Matchmaking Madness Series:

How the Lady Charmed the Marquess

How the Earl Fell for His Countess

How the Rake Tempted the Lady

How the Scot Stole the Bride

Tricking the Scoundrels Series:

Whom Shall I Kiss… An Earl, A Marquess, or A Duke?

Whom Shall I Marry… An Earl or A Duke?

I Shall Love the Earl

The Scoundrel's Wager

The Forgiven Scoundrel

Romancing the Spies Series:

Rescued By the Captain

Rescued By the Spy

Rescued By the Scot

Made in the USA
Coppell, TX
03 October 2021

63435295R00135